THE WOLVES WERE IN
THE SLEDGE

THE WOLVES WERE IN THE SLEDGE

by

STELLA GIBBONS

HODDER AND STOUGHTON

The characters in this book are entirely imaginary and
bear no relation to any living person

COPYRIGHT © 1964 *by Stella Gibbons*

FIRST PRINTED 1964

Printed in Great Britain for Hodder and Stoughton Ltd,
St. Paul's House, Warwick Lane, E.C.4,
by Hazell Watson & Viney Ltd,
Aylesbury, Bucks

TO

NOENI AND EDWARD YOUNG

I

I'VE got to have something to do. This place is getting me down.

So I've decided to write the whole thing—what happened, from the first day that I ever heard of the Rodes until now, this evening. Toby is over at the café, as usual.

I was rather good at English, at school. Original. And my father was a journalist. French, and a very *good* journalist. He came to live in England after the war, married my mother, and worked on French stories for the English papers.

He used to say—try to write exactly what you feel and see and hear. Never mind if what you write sounds ordinary, so long as the person reading can smell or hear or taste it. Just put down exactly how it is. And don't try to copy anyone else.

So that's what I'm going to do.

There was also our English mistress. Miss Moffat, known of course as The Spider. She said much the same thing, only not so plainly. She was a snooty old character but I think she did know about the English language.

Well, one evening, nearly a year ago I was lying on our bed at the Glendalyne Hotel looking at *Vogue*. It was one of those nasty cool spring evenings with dust blowing about, and it was just beginning to get dark, and I was half-enjoying *Vogue*—how I do love fashion mags—and half feeling frightened because I'd bought it and also a terrifically expensive bottle of scent.

Asia. Four pounds an ounce.

I was waving my legs in the air and wearing nothing but

7

my old red housecoat and wishing I'd been sensible and not dabbed *Asia* on myself. Because you can hide a bottle but you can't hide a delicious Chinesey-Malayan-Siamesy sort of smell, and Toby (my husband. It looks peculiar, writing "Toby, my husband" but after all he is) would be in any minute.

(I'm rather enjoying this. It brings it all back.)

She, the spidery mistress, also used to say *Don't begin every paragraph with I*. It seems the natural thing to do, and if I don't do it I shall keep on writing what looks extraordinary. But I suppose that can't be helped.

Well, now probably my name should come in.

It's Nancy Régine Leland. It used to be Nancy Régine Laforgue, I am now eighteen and a half but that evening I was seventeen and a half, and I had been married to Toby for six months.

I am—was—am, I mean—an orphan.

There was this Mrs. Raven, you see, who had this guest house in Belsize Park, Hampstead, and my father and mother were living there when I met Toby.

But they were both dead. When I met him, I mean.

My father earned quite good money, representing one or two French papers in England, and free-lancing, and he could afford to send me, first to a convent school, and then to a private school. Not expensive, but not a State one. Then one day he had to fly to Algeria on a story and there was a crash. My mother died, of a broken heart, six months later. Everyone said that was what it was.

I was still at school. Mrs. Raven was awfully kind. She took me away from school and used what money there was left to send me to a typing and shorthand school, which I loathed. The dim idea was that I should be a secretary or something.

Now I must tell the truth. Toby was a pick-up.

One evening it was raining and I was in the queue at the

8

bus-stop down in London, and a gorgeous ancient car stopped bang opposite me in the traffic jam, and in it was Toby, looking heavenly in a velvet cap, and sort-of bored. He happened to look round, and he saw me and called out "Hullo! —what luck! Can I give you a lift?"

Pretending he knew me, you see.

My father always used to say, don't talk to strange men until you are eighteen. But at the sight of Toby I forgot all the warnings.

No, that isn't true. I remembered them, in a faint sort of way, but they didn't seem to matter. I stepped out of the queue, with everyone looking fearfully jealous, and into Toby's car.

Afterwards, I found out it wasn't his at all but belonged to his friend, Guy Murray. Poor Guy.

It will be a muddle if I keep on going too far back, so now I will return to me lying on the bed at our hotel, and get on with what happened. (Oh, I must just say that in three months Toby and I got married and *where* do you think our wedding reception was held? At the *Dorchester*. Imagine. But he wouldn't let me ask Mrs. Raven because he said she is common. Also he wouldn't let me have Wendy Tucker for my bridesmaid, or write to Eileen Foster because he said they were, too.)

Suddenly the door at the Glendalyne opened and Toby came bounding in and showered pound notes all over me and started kissing me.

Kissing Toby and having him love me is *absolutely my favourite thing in the entire world*. But I don't like talking about it, and now I don't seem to like writing about it, either. So I will stop.

I said "Well?"

And Toby said, "It's all right. We're on."

9

I said—exclaimed, really—"Oh goody goody. Can we spend some of this on *eating*? I've got the Hunger Headache."

"Poor dearest," said Toby, kissing my neck. "Yes of course. Get some clothes on and we'll go to—where's the nearest decent place?"

"There's the Ballerina, just near the Wells," I said.

"That'll have to do."

My clothes are mostly black, because Toby says black suits me best. I put on a black dress and some gilt jewellery while Toby splashed himself in the little washbasin that just wasn't big enough. I was hoping he wouldn't notice the divine smell of *Asia*. I had pushed *Vogue* under the slightly grubby pillow as he came in.

But he was too excited to notice smells.

We took a taxi to the Ballerina.

The awful old Glendalyne, which was in a place called Finsbury Park in North London, was shaking away to itself as the traffic rushed past and the potplants in the enormous hall hadn't been watered for weeks (I do hate seeing plants and dogs and birds neglected) and I was delighted to be going out and spending money again.

You see, Toby had no regular job. He didn't believe in it.

Not that he was a beatnik or anything: he was at some expensive Public School with Guy, and his father is a country gentleman, a kind of hermit, who cut Toby off almost with a shilling, like someone in an ancient book, when Toby married me.

But I am going back too far again.

When we were in the Ballerina, eating steaks and drinking wine, Toby told me about these Americans, Mr. and Mrs. Rode. They wanted him to find Mr. Rode's ancestors.

They were going to be over in England for some time, depending on how things went, and they would pay him twenty guineas a week and all expenses.

It was glorious news.

The hope had been, on my part, that we should be invited to go and look for the ancestors in Italy or somewhere warm. Warmth, the sun, and sun-bathing are absolutely my favourite things, after Toby.

But no, the ancestors were in Hertfordshire.

Now I do *not* like the country. Unless you are fond of gardening there is nothing to do.

But Toby said that we should borrow Guy's car, The Car, as we all called it, and there would be all kinds of perks in the way of delicious meals at expensive country pubs, and no doubt theatres and bits off tailors' and restaurant bills if Toby introduced these rich Americans there, and altogether he thought that for the next few months we should have a very nice time. To say nothing of the twenty guineas a week.

"Goody goody," I said again, drinking wine and thinking how divinely blue Toby's eyes are—long and narrow, with eyelashes like a little boy's. He is also very tall and very slim. Absolutely gorgeous in fact.

And then of course he suddenly sniffed the air and said, "Good God, what's that stuff you've got on?"

He had got wise to *Asia*.

"It's only scent," I said, with a sinking stomach. (How extraordinary that looks. *Stomach*.)

"It must have cost the earth."

I didn't say anything.

"How much did it cost, Nancy?"

It was no use. I had to tell him.

"Four pounds."

He didn't suppose it was a big bottle, either. Toby knows about expensive scents and wines and things. He has to, because of the kind of people he likes us—him and me—to be friends with. (Well, not what you would really call friends, I suppose.)

"Four pounds an ounce. You've been at the Reserve Fund again, Nancy. It's too bad of you."

The Reserve Fund was five guineas. (Toby says the name *guineas* cheers him up more than *pounds*.) Some money came to Toby every month, and I supposed it was from Investments. Five guineas of it was always kept in a pocket-book in his suitcase, for times when we were really desperate.

"I shall have to keep it myself, in future," he said, in the cool voice that makes me miserable.

"I'm truly sorry, Toby. But I just can't resist scent."

"I suppose you can't be expected to behave as if you'd been to a decent school," he went on, as if I hadn't spoken, "Girls who have, take some things for granted."

"Well I took four pounds, and if you're so keen on girls who've been to decent schools, why did you marry me?"

"You know why," he said, and then I laughed and he laughed, and it was all right.

But I knew that he would take over the Reserve Fund, and keep it hidden, in future. When it comes to managing me, Toby can be firm.

But talking about decent schools seemed to have started him thinking about Guy.

"My *God*, we're lucky to have Guy," he said in a thankful sort of voice like someone mentioning a saint.

I wanted to say "Why?" or "Are we?" but instead I only nodded. One thing I had learnt thoroughly in being married to Toby for six months was when to keep quiet about Guy. But it hadn't stopped me being jealous of him.

"He introduced me to these people. They don't know anyone else in England."

"How does he come to know them?" I asked, trying to sound interested.

"Their son was over here in the American Air Force some years ago, and Guy met him then. (He was a motor-racing fan.) Then he was killed in Korea and Guy wrote to them. So when they decided to come over, of course he was the one person they wanted to see."

I nodded again, and asked if they were rich.

"Oh yes. Not rolling but more than easy. You'll meet them tomorrow : we're lunching with them."

Now this really was happy news. Two good hot meals two days running.

"Where?" I asked. Toby had once taken me to the Caprice. The scampi, and the hats! I still day-dreamed about that lunch.

"A funny old place in Macomber Street called The Chandos. It's wonderfully tatty. It used to be run by a *poule-de-luxe*, between the Wars."

"It doesn't sound like a rich place," I said, disappointed.

"It isn't. It's deliberately quaint, to attract Americans. The food is bearable but no more. Never mind, poppet, I'll take you somewhere gorgeous soon." He stood up and reached for his coat, hanging on a peg behind him. "No time for coffee. Come along."

"Where to?" I asked, disappointed.

"Guy knows a character who's going to lend us a flat in Hampstead."

"Oh, near Belsize Park? Goody goody."

"It's on the other side, behind John Barnes's shop. And no running round to see Ma Raven," Toby said crushingly. "We'll move in tonight. Guy's going over there to open it up for us. *Marche*, Idle!" and he strode between the table to the cash desk.

I snatched up my coat and bag and followed. It was only eight o'clock now, and I was excited at the idea of having a flat to ourselves. Even with Guy hanging about and staring at me, it would be fun.

II

I AM beginning to see that when you are writing something it can't go rushing on anyhow. You have to divide it up, to give whoever's reading it a rest. So I have put II at the top of the page.

You see, Toby and I had never had our own home. Toby had no money to buy one. Besides, he didn't believe in having one, not all the time, with furniture, and a number on the gate and that kind of thing. He said it was stifling. And I suppose I was too young to want one. At seventeen, you enjoy rushing about.

So we used to borrow someone's studio for a few days, or stay with someone we'd picked up at a rich party, or go to a cheap hotel like the Glendalyne. All our money—the Reserve Fund, that is, because I hadn't any money and had never even had a job to earn any—all our money went on our clothes, and *suitcases*.

Toby was serious about luggage. Cheap cases made him feel really bad. He said they marked you for life. If you turned up in a new place with a fibre case—unless you were some titled person of course—you had had it, and there was no way out except to get colossally rich or be a duke and then you could carry your things round in paper bags if you wanted to.

As for clothes, we both practically worshipped them. They were our passion. We spent hours window-shopping for them, and the few ones we had were very good, and Toby made me take great care of them.

I was always trotting round to the cleaners or the invisible mending place. I can mend very well, my mother taught me, but sometimes even my mending isn't good enough for Toby.

Toby told me what to wear, too, and how to have my hair cut—it's dark red, and it slightly curls—and he chose my hats. He says only undistinguished little girls don't wear a hat.

Well, on this evening we went back to the poor old Glendalyne and Toby packed.

He does it beautifully, with sheets of fresh tissue paper that he keeps specially. I stand beside him folding the clothes and occasionally being cursed for doing it wrong, and at last our two beautiful suitcases and the box for my hat-of-the-moment—I only have one at a time—were ready, and shut.

Toby paid our bill, and the ghastly old woman at the desk with dyed hair and a mouth like a rat-trap——

But was it? I was going to write that without thinking. I've never seen a rat-trap that looked like her mouth. I've never seen a rat-trap at all, in fact.

No, it was like nothing but a sad straight painted old mouth, really. (It shows how you can be led away while you are writing.)

Well, she took the money without a glance at either of us, and we went out of the Glendalyne into the spring night and found a taxi.

Hampstead has lovely little shops. Mostly antique or coffee-bars. They were all lit up and softly shining as our taxi climbed the hill and I was sorry when it turned down Fitz-john's Avenue—the Park Lane of North London, they used to call it, Mum used to say—and into Finchley Road.

Rowland Mansions were definitely a disappointment. I'd taken it for granted that a friend of Guy's would live in a luxury block. But although there was one just opposite, Rowland Mansions was a tall thin grey brick place, with a kind of parapet at the top and looking definitely gone to seed.

15

However, out we got, and the taxi-driver wouldn't help us up the stairs with our cases to No. 16 because he said he had a weak heart.

Toby is always nice to taxi-drivers and people. He says it softens his path through life and is more well-bred.

He let the taxi-driver talk about his heart for a bit, and even listened without fidgeting while he went on to tell us about Rowland Mansions, how they had just been taken over by a new company, which was trying to get the tenants out so that they could convert the flats into luxury ones.

"They'll need a good deal done to them," said Toby, looking up at broken windows, and the staircase all over bits of newspaper and dust, and paint peeling off.

"Ar, I believe you," said the driver, "but this new lot's got plenty. They'll make a nice job out of them, they will, once they get the old tenants out."

Toby gave him a good tip—that's another thing he believes in, tipping well, though he says never overdo it or they think you're frightened.

"I let him chat on," he said, as we climbed slowly up the stairs with our heavy cases, "because it may come in useful to know something about the place."

Toby is like that. Always looking ahead. It makes me feel so safe with him (not that I get alarmed about things, anyway but this looking ahead kind of takes the place of his having a regular job and so forth).

I really only get alarmed at *one thing* and that is *big dogs*, and suddenly just as we were stopping on a dusty landing to have a bit of a rest, there was the most dreadful bark, a very deep throaty growling one, and I gave a loud scream.

"Don't do that, Nancy," said Toby, but in his "awful" voice, and put his arm round me. We both looked towards the door where the sound came from. (He doesn't like me fearing big dogs because he says it's un-English and common.)

16

It was painted a lovely dark red and all the knockers and things glittered as if they were in full sunlight. It looked rich. On the way up the other doors had their glass panels broken and boarded over with cardboard or badly needed painting but this one really cheered you up.

"Someone must have a bit of money, good," whispered Toby, and we staggered on up the stairs. That dog didn't bark again.

Just as we got to the top we heard Guy whistling.

He had a splendid whistle—loud and clear and true. It always made me think of the birds in the garden, in the mornings at Belsize Park.

Then he opened the door and came running to help us with our cases.

"Hullo, hullo, hullo," he almost shouted, "welcome home." He seized my case. "How are they all at The Moorings?"

This was an absolutely imaginary place he and Toby were supposed to know, in the country. A kind of old clergyman was imagined to live in it with a lot of daughters, and Guy and Toby always said, "What would they say at The Moorings?" whenever they thought of some new plan. It had been going on for years, they told me. I never thought it was funny.

"Oh, tolerable," said Toby. "Henrietta's headaches have returned."

"Who can wonder?" said Guy, and held back the door for me to go in, staring.

He always stared at me, so I was used to it.

There was a little hall, papered in dark red, not a rich cheerful one like the door downstairs but kind-of gloomy. Dark blue fitted carpet, quite new. Doors, all shut, painted pale grey. No pictures on the walls, no stand for a clothes brush, nothing but a row of gilt pegs for hats and things. All quiet, awfully quiet, and rather stuffy.

"Living-room—bedroom—dining-room—bathroom—loo,"

Guy was calling out, opening one door after another. "Box-room, opening out of bedroom."

"I like this," said Toby, meaning a queer little sort of plat-form with two steps in the living-room.

The steps were under a little round window like one in a ship set high in the wall and Toby ran up them and opened it. The wind came in and blew up his hair. (It's like brown embroidery-silk.)

"Smells good," he said, "nice view of roofs."

I was looking round. I didn't like the room. I didn't like it right from the beginning. It was all done in red like the corri-dor, with no ornaments except a sort of ball in a metal frame on the mantelpiece, and it was so quiet. Even with our voices, it felt quiet.

"What's that?" I asked Guy, pointing.

"That's an orrery, darling Nancy."

He always called me that. I didn't like it. Perhaps because I was jealous of him.

"What's an orrery?" I repeated the word carefully.

Guy explained. But I won't put that in, as you can always look up the word in a dictionary.

"I say—gorgeous shirts!" Toby was shouting from the next room. "Who *is* your friend, Guy?"

"Oh . . . a man I knew at Oriel. The adventurous type," Guy said, lying full length on a red sofa, with his eyes half-shut. But looking, as usual, at me.

"Didn't you say he'd gone abroad. If so, he won't need all these shirts." Toby came in with a shirt held up against him-self, looking gorgeous. "There must be thirty of them."

"He's gone to Algeria. I should assume that he won't re-turn," said Guy.

Here I suppose I ought to tell how Guy looked. It does make it more interesting.

He was shorter than Toby, and sturdy, while Toby is the

18

slim type. Guy had very dark brown hair, almost reddish, which would curl if allowed, and eyes the colour of a dark sherry. It was a square, cheerful face, and while Toby usually looked bored, Guy usually looked amused.

I can see his face clearly. I put my Biro down, just here, and tried whether I could, and I can, very clearly. It was a face that could change quickly in expression, and sometimes I felt that it could show all kinds of expressions which you hadn't imagined he could feel.

That is muddly. I am sorry. And usually Guy's face seemed nothing more than cheerfully amused, with those heavy eyelids that can be looked from under without seeming to.

He was a very famous racing-motorist, world-famous. But just now he was out of a regular job because he had quarrelled with the firm he tried out cars for. (Toby said it was not a quarrel but a disagreement, in which Guy was dead right. But it came to the same thing.)

This was bad news for me, as Guy would now have lots of spare time to be with Toby. I was very jealous, that first evening in Rowland Mansions.

Toby came back, looking heavenly in one of the Orielman's shirts, and if we had been alone I would have made him kiss me, which is never a difficult task. But of course we had to have Guy there, lolling all over the sofa and staring at me. No particular expression. Just staring, between those eyelids.

Suddenly there came a loud, thin, crazy mewing from somewhere.

"What is this place—an annexe of the Zoo?" Toby cried frantically—he hates animals and only makes up to them sometimes because he says they can be useful socially—they make a mess, he says, and are boring.

"It's a kitten." Guy got off the sofa and went to the box-room. "I forgot—it was in here when I came, I think it's starving."

"Oh, my God," said Toby, sitting down on the sofa.

I followed Guy. I don't much like animals either—I suppose it's my French blood—but I hate, as I have said, to see things neglected.

The kitten came staggering out of the boxroom when we opened the door. It had a sort of crazed look in its very blue eyes. It was absolutely snow-white and fearfully thin.

"I know," . . . said Guy who had picked it up and was letting it eat his finger, "Toby, you go down and ask old Pegram for some milk."

"And who is old Pegram?" Toby came sauntering in and looked hatingly at the kitchen.

"One floor down—red door. His grandfather built this block and he has a gent's agreement that he stays on here whatever happens to the place. You go down and borrow some milk."

"Why?" asked Toby in his lazy voice.

"May come in useful," said Guy.

These words, and all that silliness about The Moorings were what I most often heard Toby and Guy say. And when they, the former, were spoken, both would always obey what the other suggested. So, picking up the kitten by its neck, down Toby went holding it out stiffly in front of him.

"I hope you weren't frightened by that dog, darling Nancy," said Guy, coming to stand at the bedroom door to watch me unpacking our cases, "because it doesn't exist. That is, it does, but what you heard was a gramophone record."

I looked up, surprised, and he nodded.

"Old Pegram had it made, to scare people off."

"Why should he want to do that?"

"Well"—Guy hesitated—"the new owners. He's being obstinate about getting out, and they've had to adopt certain lines of attack."

20

"What sort of lines?" (Bullying the old thing, I thought. My father used to say that I had "the typical quickness of the feminine mind about personal situations".)

"Oh . . . just certain lines. Not particularly interesting . . . Will you both come out to dinner with me? and we'll go on to The Darling Daughter."

This is a pub, down on the river in the East End, where we sometimes go. I love it.

"We've had dinner, thank you. But I expect Toby'd adore to go to The Daughter."

"Then I'll get something there. Hurry up."

"He's rather a nice old cocksparrow," said Toby, coming back. "Stands about five feet in his slippers. Asked me in. A lot of swords and Indian tat about—was he in the Army?"

"Regulars. Chucked out a few years ago. But he has something put aside, I imagine, and his pension. Where's the little cat?"

"Oh, that caused tremendous excitement. It belongs to Miss de Havilland, who lives another floor down. It's been missing for days and 'you know what old maids are about cats'. Idle, it's your turn." He pulled the kitten, with its face all over milk, out of his pocket, squealing and scratching. "Down you go. Number twelve."

"Why couldn't he take it himself?" I said, grumbling.

"Afraid I might be an emissary from the new owners, I think, and dart in and lock him out. Anyway, it might come in useful to know Miss de Havilland."

That was because she had "de" in front of her name. Toby could never resist it.

I went downstairs, clutching the kitten. It felt all bones and claws.

You may think it extraordinary that I can remember exactly what we said, after nearly a year ago. Well of course I can't. But I do remember what happened, and, more or less, what we said. I remember it because, from that first evening of ever hearing about the Rodes, my life began to become what might be called more serious.

But I will go back to Rowland Mansions. (I like remembering it. Life was fun in those days. I took it obsolutely for granted, too, all those blessings of civilisation. But I must get on.)

Miss de Havilland opened the door to me. She was about ninety, I should think. Her face was like a brown nut, with white hair screwed up under a *hat*, and she had a lovely lace blouse under a really good jersey suit—skirt five inches too long. Fifteen years old, I should think. Those things *last*.

"Oh—Snowy!" she said loudly. "*How* kind of you," taking him from me, "where did you find him?"

I explained, and had to stop and listen while she told me that he must have wormed his way along a balcony or something and got in, over the roof, by that little round window which then banged shut, imprisoning him like a human being in a story.

I tried to look interested, because Toby had said she might come in useful, and he does so like knowing people with "de" names. At last she said I must come to tea with her one day, and thanked me again, and Snowy looked hatingly at me, and I could get away.

She didn't seem a bit interested in who I was or where we'd come from, which was a blessing.

"Did you get a chance to mention Aunt Hermy?" said Toby casually, when I got back.

"No. I could hardly get a word in anyway. And I couldn't interrupt her and shout 'My husband has an aunt named Lady South who lives in a Keep in Essex,' could I?"

"I suppose not," said Toby. But he looked disappointed. These details mean a great deal to him, as being part of his life's plan for getting us on in the world. I said that I would

22

bring in Aunt Hermy when I went to tea with Miss de Havilland and he told me not to forget and I promised.

Then Guy shouted to us to hurry up and we ran down the stairs and got into his car—"My wife"—he calls it—which is a gorgeous old one, built in 1935, and went off to The Darling Daughter. We didn't get home until four. It was rather nice to come back to a place you could think of as home, in spite of my not liking that place.

Happy days.

III

THE next morning it was agony getting up.

I adore sleeping. Bed is my favourite place. But Toby woke me, shaking me, and saying had I forgotten we were lunching with the Rodes, and it was eight o'clock, and I must look absolutely my best and have my hair done.

"It was done the day before yesterday," I mumbled.

"I know, pet, and I adore it." He put his face into it. "You still smell of that stuff. But you really must look extra gorgeous to-day. This may be our big chance."

This was one of the things that Toby said often. I wasn't quite sure what our big chance meant, exactly, except that someone rich would practically adopt us and take us to live with them in a huge luxurious house in a warm place far away.

Often, too, Toby's first words when he woke up were "If only I could get my hands on some real money!" But I think he would have been satisfied with quite a little money really, so long as the *background*, if you know what I mean, was all there—warmth, and people with "de" names, and luxury.

Myself, I am not so mad for luxury. So long as it's warm, and people are cheerful, and nothing is being neglected, I don't mind quite a poor sort of place. Toby had to talk to me seriously, when we were first married, about having *higher standards*.

Said I was too easily pleased.

I always remember, when I had known him about three weeks and was getting really crazy about him, he made me stop wearing a dress my mother had carefully chosen for me,

24

which was quite expensive, because he said it was the colour of *dou-dou*, and fake *diamanté* clips were the ultimate and final *end*.

He told me to burn the dress and gave me the money for a plain black one, in floaty chiffon.

The other dress was sold by me to Mrs. Raven's daughter and I remember being for a second actually relieved that Mum was dead because her feelings couldn't be hurt by my refusing to wear what she had chosen.

She always said that being married to a Frenchman had quite changed her ideas about clothes. But Toby said it hadn't, and I don't really think it had.

Of course—to return to my *standards*—I adore divine clothes and delicious food. But I don't feel a sort of craving to have them all the time for myself. If I come to think about it, if I can have a good hot meal once a day, and the weather is warm, I am contented.

Toby says "contented" is a dirty word.

Well, I crept up, and into my black nylon housecoat, and we had coffee, and then I went out and was lucky enough to find a hairdresser with time to fit me in.

When I got back, Toby was shaved and looking divine in another of Oriel-man's shirts.

"I say, are you sure that's all right?" I asked, because I was only just learning not to be what Toby calls "hopelessly middle-class" about borrowing people's things without them knowing and so forth.

"Will you kindly leave things to me, Nancy," he said— jumpy, you see, because this lunch might be the beginning of our big chance. When he calls me by my name it means he is nervous and therefore cross.

So I didn't say another word, though I would have liked some kissing, as Oriel-man's shirt certainly did set off Toby's looks, and then we went down to The Car, which Guy had let us have.

On the way down the gloomy stairs we ran into a fight.

There was Miss de Havilland, in her hat and lace blouse, and a little old gentleman with a red face and a moustache, standing in the middle of a lot of shouting children.

The children had educated voices, but they were being frightfully rude, and shouting "Oldies! Oldies!" and threatening the old people with water-pistols.

Toby silently swooped down on them with his long arms stretched out and they shrieked and rushed away down the stairs, half-laughing but a bit frightened too, and Toby gently asked Miss de Havilland if she was all right?

She was sitting on the stairs, gasping a little, and her face was a queer colour.

"Heart—heart," said the little old gentleman, taking off his hat to me and slightly bowing in a cross way, "the little brutes do this every time one of us comes out to do a bit of shopping or take a walk. It's my firm belief the new owners are behind it. Tipping them half-a-crown each. Anything to get us out, eh, Miss de Havilland? 'Disgraceful' is too weak a word for it." He settled his cuffs and shopping-bag and stick, fussily. Miss de Havilland nodded.

"May I see you to your door?" Toby was saying to her.

It was a good thing that we were in plenty of time. Otherwise, he would have had to choose between being nice to these two old people, who might 'come in useful', and being late for lunch with the Rodes.

"I am better now, thank you." She stood up, brushing dust and grit from that long skirt. "The poor little creatures live in those new flats opposite—all the parents seem to have money and are all strict Pagans, of course—and there may be something in what Mr. Pegram says. It really amounts to a persecution, does it not?"

26

Mr. Pegram nodded in gloomy silence.

"Well, we must not keep you," said Miss de Havilland. "Thank you for your kindly help."

So we went on down the stairs, leaving them there.

"Toby, is a Pagan the same as a heathen?"

"Oh my God, Nancy, I do sometimes wish you'd been to a moderately good school."

"I did go to the convent until I was eight. And I only wanted to know," I said, in a peaceful voice. "The nuns had a reputation for being very clever."

"Or even had a—a—normally retentive brain."

"I am normal," I said, still in a peaceful voice but in myself feeling a bit insulted. Nobody likes to be called abnormal.

"Of course you are. Don't be so touchy—why are women always so personal?—I simply meant—oh never mind what I meant—and *don't take your hat off*—"

"The straw's scratching my forehead."

"Oh God, the difficulties of my life. Get in, please."

Still feeling jumpy, you see.

I settled myself beside him, saying "retentive" over in my mind and determined to buy a dictionary in secret, and look it up. (I did, too.)

Never in my whole life, until of course we came here, had I seen anywhere so worn out and shabby as the Chandos Hotel in Macomber Street, W.1.

It had a wide dark doorway above three steps with the marble broken away, and some of the letters in its name had fallen down so that it read like " NDOS OTEL".

Macomber Street seemed to have done what Toby would call "run down", too. There were two restaurants that smelt of chips frying (though I like chips) and a shop with dresses in the wrong kind of bright colours, all in the middle of good-looking quiet little shops selling tweeds and hand-made pipes and scent and things, for rich well-connected people.

27

The Chandos's entrance hall was dim and gloomy with huge pictures of dead birds and stags being eaten by herds of wolves on the walls, and old Persian carpets simply worn into strings and very dangerous.

You could see into rooms full of old sofas and chairs and silver photo frames and more worn carpets. It was all as quiet as *doom.*

"How much a week do they charge here, for godssake?" I whispered, as we waited while an old lady in a long tweed skirt with snow white hair walked slowly away to find the Rodes. "Is that the receptionist?"

"Do *not* say 'for godssake', Nancy. It sounds like Ma Raven."

"She used to say it."

"Well, don't you say it. It's terrible. I don't know. But it isn't cheap."

"Why aren't they at the Dorchester or the Westbury?"

"I suppose because this is English and quaint. Shut up, now."

I had my black shantung suit and I smelt of jasmine this morning, but I couldn't feel cheerful. What would lunch be like? I was starving. And the Rodes? Suppose they were ghastly? We had to live off them, Toby had said, for the next few months.

Well, here they came.

Slowly, out of the dim passage leading away into the back part of the Chandos Hotel, Mr. Rode walking ahead and Mrs. Rode a little way behind.

They came up to us and Mr. Rode shook hands with Toby and Mrs. Rode took both my hands between hers in expensive-looking pink gloves, and squeezed them.

"Why, you're just as I imagined you would be," she said, smiling.

Now what do I say to that? I didn't know many old people.

28

or I would have remembered they are always imagining about you. (Not that she was awfully old; about fifty-two, I should think.)

So I just smiled and said nothing, and Mr. Rode said he was sure we were both hungry, so come along. Toby was cleverly making conversation.

Away we trailed, walking slowly because Mr. Rode was a tall slow wandery kind of man—with a face rather like a thoughtful horse—and Mrs. Rode had tight shoes. She was almost hobbling.

They were on the smallest feet I've ever seen.

I take a four, which is small for nowadays I'm told, but I should think she took a *three*, if you could get them, and she was trying to wear a *two*.

Now my father always said that those very managing women, who make men do what they want without seeming to, take a size two in shoes. So I was on my guard. Because I was not going to have Mrs. Rode managing me.

No doubt this seems touchy at a first interview. But I get quite enough being managed by angel Toby, without having anyone else doing it, and I have had to learn how to stop people before they start, kind-of.

They were easy to get on with, thank goodness.

I just said all the perfectly ordinary things that came into my head, about The Chandos (not quite what came into my head there) and the weather, and then clothes—Mrs Rode admired my suit—and chattered away.

Toby talked to Mr. Rode most of the time, working hard. I have seen him doing this lots of times in the past six months, and now I know that he was working hard when he used to tell me about himself before we were even married.

It isn't exactly telling lies. It is more like making a picture, so that the other person shall see him as he wants them to.

Mrs. Rode was asking me if I spoke French? "Your husband told us you are half French," she said.

"Yes," I answered her, in my father's language, "I always talked French with my father, he only died last year." I still could not say this without deep pain.

Mrs. Rode gave a tinkling sort of laugh. "That sounds so pretty," she said. "Now let me see if I can translate."

Out of one ear I could hear Toby and Mr. Rode getting serious about ordering the wine, and now a waitress came doddering up.

The receptionist's hair had been in a bun. This one had a perm and a very short skirt. But it made no difference. She must have been quite seventy.

"The wine waiter, please," said Mr. Rode, as if he would be brought in on a tray.

"There isn't a wine-waiter, sir. Mr. Elphinstone, he was the last one, he was here in Mrs. Hereford's time, he died last year," said the waitress.

"That's too bad," said Mr. Rode, "was he an elderly man?"

I guessed that he was, myself, and sure enough the waitress said he was eighty—and quite a part of the place.

"And they never replaced him," she ended up.

"Is that so?" Mr. Rode was keeping his eyes behind huge horn-rimmed spectacles fixed on her face, but I couldn't make out whether he was being nice, or interested in this bit of English quaintness, or impatient, or what. His face usually looked just thoughtful.

"The Prince of Wales—Duke of Windsor he is now—used to dine here frequent just after the war, and he always asked for Mr. Elphinstone," the waitress said.

I could feel Toby getting impatient. He hates being held up.

"The Duke hasn't lived in London since 1935," he said sharply.

30

"The 1914 War, sir, I meant. In the twenties, it would be," said the waitress, in a respectfully triumphant kind of voice.

"Well, I suppose you do have a wine list—unless that was discontinued when Mr. Elphinstone left us?" said Mr. Rode.

"Oh yes, sir. Shall I bring it, sir?"

"If you please."

Mr. Rode leant back in his chair and said "Whew!" Mrs. Rode said it was all delightfully quaint and English wasn't it, and Toby smiled at the little joke about Mr. E., but I knew he was irritated.

He may think it *useful* to have Americans like our quaint old ways, but he doesn't at all like it when they get annoyed at them.

He gets worked up about England being corny, and a second-rate power. He likes to think of England as clever at science, and designing those huge aeroplanes the Government is always spending twenty million on and then deciding not to have after all.

He hates what he calls quaintery.

(Of course, I don't feel like this about England because I don't think of myself as English.)

But when the wine came at last he and Mr. Rode were both surprised. It was good.

I didn't notice what it was. Toby once told me good wine was wasted on me because I enjoy any kind of old plum-juice. I can t help that. We drank wine at home without thinking.

"Now," said Mr. Rode, "we must drink to the occasion." He lifted his glass. "To the Rode-Leland Ancestor-Hunting Company, Incorporated."

We all held up our glasses and said the words after him, and drank.

No-one took any notice. All round us, in that dining-room the size of a small church with long windows looking out

31

on to a stony little yard full of dusty plants, people were sitting at the tables. And their faces!

Real old English faces, proud and nose-y and calm. Their hats looked as if they had been *built* for the old women wearing them—velvet, and peculiar flowers, and even hat-pins.

They didn't care, you see. They were themselves, and fashion and that sort of thing, just didn't come into it.

"Ah—pease-pudding," said Toby when the waitress brought our food, "we always had that when I went to stay with Aunt Hermy."

(I had been expecting her to come up.)

The Rodes looked interested.

"Lady South. ('Hermy' is short for Hermione.) She has an enchanting old castle in Essex—Abbotstower. She had the Keep made into a flat—been there for years now, since I was a little boy—"

"Can that be so long ago?" said Mrs. Rode with a motherly smile.

Now, Toby is twenty-six. I have not put this in before simply because I know he minds it, and I am writing as though someone was going to read it, and would then learn his little weakness.

And after all twenty-six *is* quite old.

He smiled a quick, annoyed smile and went on—"I used to adore going there to stay."

"Indeed. Perhaps we shall have the pleasure of driving over there one day. Mrs. Rode dearly loves a historical building," Mr. Rode said.

"I'd be delighted to show you over it, sir. But my aunt doesn't live there except for a few weeks in the summer. She lets the place now and has her home in the South of France, on her doctor's advice."

So that disposed of that. I'd never met Aunt Hermy nor Toby's father nor any of his family, because of their being

32

furious when Toby married me. I suppose they wanted him to marry someone with a title or masses of money. He had never told me why they were furious, just that they were.

I can't say that I minded much. So long as I had Toby I used not to mind anything.

Well, this lunch went on, with me enjoying the food which was really quite good, considering the gone-to-seedness of the Chandos Hotel, and Toby getting into a story he always tells new rich people we meet about Aunt Hermy's father who used to have one of the Kings—I never can remember whether it was the one who gave up his throne to marry that Duchess of Windsor or another one who was old and plump and rather gay—who called champagne "a bottle of the boy".

The point was that this particular King used to go shooting with Toby's Aunt Hermy's grandfather. So it reflected well on Toby, you see.

The Rhodes liked this story, I could see. And now I suppose you would like to know how Mrs. Rode looked. (I always think that makes a thing more interesting. I remember once someone lending me a book where there wasn't one single word about how people looked, but only how they talked, and I had to put it down.)

Mrs. Rode was short and plump and you got an overall impression of veils and flowers and cream-colour and pinkishness and sparkling dressmaker jewellery, original and wonderfully smart. I think it was by Dior.

She looked like someone of over fifty who had never stopped being a girl, if you know what I mean. In her clothes, and her mind, and everything. But I mean the out-of-date kind of girl, who washed, and was light-hearted, and adored scent and frills. (Though frills are in again, this year.) Mrs. Rode was *youthful*, but, in spite of the jewellery, not smart.

Afterwards, when I thought I was getting to know her better, I found that she was cheerful, and never said that anything was a serious problem. She was always ready to enjoy things.

Now that is something I like very much.

Of course, I suppose having a lot of money makes it easy to be cheerful. But I don't know.

Mrs. Rode's name was Marybelle, which I think is pretty, though Toby groaned later on about it and said it was just what you would have expected. Mr. Rode's name was Clay, which I think is a simply awful name and I don't know how anyone could bear to be called it. Mrs. Rode called him "Honeybug" which I thought was sweet and he called her "Honeybug" as well.

Soon we were drinking our coffee and brandy—the old waitress brought along a brandy which Toby said was "worthy of the deepest veneration".

(I still remembered about "retentive" and that dictionary, and I made an inward note about "veneration" too. Sometimes Toby is pleased when I ask him what words mean and sometimes he is cross.

He says, how do I remember every single word he ever says and how people look and their hats and things and yet know only about eight words and all of them ordinary? Angel Toby.)

It was arranged that we should call for the Rhodes the next morning at ten o'clock and drive them out to this place Waltham Abbey where Mr. Rode had had an ancestor. Toby said he would call for them in The Car and went on to say the piece about it that he always does, about her being thirty years old and the love of his life. As if it really was his.

Mrs. Rode laughed across at me and said, "Are you jealous, Nancy?"

"Not a bit," I said. It was a good thing she hadn't asked me if I was jealous of the car's real owner.

I must say that Guy is very kind about letting Toby borrow

34

The Car. He does let Toby pay him something, of course, but if I loved anything as much as Guy loves The Car I wouldn't lend it to anyone. But I suppose girls are different.

Guy is fond of money, I think. That's why he lets Toby pay him, which seems funny, when they are such great friends.

Toby asked Mr. Rode if there would be much to go on, in this ancestor hunting.

"I have been drawing out a family tree for the last ten years," said Mr. Rode, "with names, and dates But unfortunately my chief source of supply was destroyed when my Aunt Minna of Newstream, Maine, died last year. I was in the West on business at the time, and some chuckleheaded busybody burned a whole heap of papers before anyone in authority could stop her. With the material I've worked up at home, we can go back as far as Jabez Rode, married to Maria Watts in this place Waltham Abbey, some time in the mid seventeen hundreds. She lived in the village."

"Waltham Abbey goes back to the time of Harold—the one who was killed at the battle of Hastings," said Toby.

"Ten sixty-six," I interrupted because this is one of the dates I can remember, and Toby looked at me furiously, as if I had said something silly and went on—"he founded the place."

"I shall dearly love to see the Abbey," said Mrs. Rode, "we must take a whole heap of pictures."

"That will just suit Marybelle," said Mr. Rode, looking at her in a teasing way, "she loves a historical building. She's the romantic type."

"I am not, so!" said Mrs. Rode. Teasing each other, you see. Like Toby and me. They *were* easy to get on with, I was going to like them, I thought, and I hoped Toby would as well. He really can be depressing when he can't like people for any reason. Poor people for instance or people with problems or ailments.

35

Sometimes I think the only people he really does like are me and Guy.

"We're going to have *fun*!" Mrs. Rode said to me, sparkling —no, I think dimplifying is a truer word—all over her face as we all said goodbye, and I was starting to agree with her.

IV

THE next morning I went to sleep again while Toby was having his bath and he was furious and we had a mad rush to get ready and he wouldn't speak to me all the way down into London.

But thanks to luck we got there punctually and the Rodes weren't even ready. So Toby filled in time while we were sitting in The Car outside the Chandos by giving me a ticking-off.

Said I didn't back him up in his efforts to get us on in the world.

"How don't I? I do everything I'm told."

"You put your creature comforts first."

"I do not."

"You do, Nancy. Take this morning—just for a few extra minutes in bed you risked losing what may be our big chance."

"I couldn't help falling asleep again, could I?"

"Yes you could. What you never realize is that getting on isn't a question of luck, or being a charmer. It needs *damned hard work* with every bit of you looking out, and on its toes. You can't just slop at it."

Fortunately at that moment the Rodes came out, looking just the same as yesterday.

Waltham Abbey is only about twelve miles from London but Toby reckoned it would take us more than an hour to get there because of the traffic. So off we went, me at the back with Mrs. R. and Toby in front with Mr.

I don't mind traffic, being a person who enjoys crowds, but

Toby hates to be held up and I could see his long fair face under his angelic velvet cap getting crosser and crosser though he was trying not to show it. Mr. R. talked to him about American things and I could see that they were used to a high standard of living.

Mrs. R. talked to me about her dead son, and her daughter-in-law, Ruth. It was a great sorrow to her that poor Ruth hadn't started a baby before the son was killed in wherever-it-was, because then Mrs. R. would have had a grandchild.

"I expect you are longing for your first, aren't you, honey?" she said to me. Kindly, but I didn't know what to say.

Because I am not longing for a baby at all. I once stayed for a week-end with a school-friend who was married and had one (Toby had gone to stay with some rich friend of his former life) and truly and solemnly I shall never forget those three days and the awfulness of them.

Why, the baby never let its mother alone for a single minute. Even when it was asleep there were things to be done for it. She was nothing but a slave. And yet she seemed to love the baby. But it cured me of ever wanting one. So long as I can have Toby to myself, I don't want anyone else.

So when Mrs. R. said that, I only smiled, and she soon turned to the more cheerful subject of clothes.

I will not describe our boring journey, but there was one bit which I will describe, because I remember it clearly.

It was a bit of old countryside left in the middle of suburbia, really, a green cornfield sloping down a placid hill, with some big trees on the top and an old red and grey farmhouse and some barns. One of them had a silvery thatched roof, and black birds were walking about, in the green corn, cawing to themselves.

I just put down my Biro and sat back, remembering. That ordinary little piece of Epping Forest, which now seems like a paradise. Yet we took it quite for granted. Mrs. R. did say it was pretty, but that was all.

Well, soon we were in Waltham Abbey.

It is an absolutely ordinary English village, old but spoilt, not all by itself in deep country but joined on to Waltham Cross by a main road and traffic rushes through it by day and by night too, I expect. There are all kinds of shops—but no Woolworths—which I cannot help liking.

Toby parked The Car on the edge of a yard advertising tours to Essex beauty spots, where a man came out of a little office and stared at it.

Toby said to Mr. Rode:

"Now, sir, I suggest that we make for the nearest church and ask to see their Register of Marriages."

"There's one," I said, pointing down a street of little old houses.

"Good—we'll make for that," said Toby and off we went.

Mrs. R.'s shoes had low heels to-day, suitable for the country, and she wasn't hobbling. I approved of her sensible-ness.

After I had spoken, I wasn't sure if it really was a church because it hadn't a spire and didn't look churchy, it had a sort of large porch almost like a Greek temple and a bit sticking up from that like a scooped out pyramid, if you know how I mean. It stood in its own grounds, with a lot of tombstones all crowded together in long very green grass. Hadn't been cut for weeks. It all looked deserted.

"What shall we do?" I asked, when we had stared at it for a bit.

"Find the vicar," said Toby, "the name is on that board over there."

So he and Mr. Rode went off, and Mrs. Rode sat down on a tombstone in the sun and smiled up at me.

"Having fun?" she asked, and I smiled and nodded.

39

But I wasn't sure.

I don't like churches. The sky was azure (that's a pretty word, I found it in a fashion mag) and the wind warm and soft but somehow that quiet little church made you feel quiet too. I was brought up as a Catholic, which my father was, but he was *croyant*, not *pratiquante*, and I am not particularly even *croyante*. I always tell myself there's plenty of time for thinking about these things when I am old. And I don't like feeling quiet in that sort of way.

And here came Toby and Mr. Rode with a long thin man in very white shirtsleeves.

"We're in luck," Toby called, "Mr. Hanks was in his garden. He's the verger."

"I don't know— —" Mr. Hanks, the tall thin man, was saying doubtfully, "Mr. Benson being away—the last thing he said to me was 'don't unlock the church between services,' he said, 'I'm tired of asking the P.C.C. for money for new boxes for the U.M.C.A. and the Restoration and the Flowers and all the rest,' he said. You get all sorts, nowadays."

"Do we look like types that break open church boxes?" Toby asked, rather crossly.

"How do I know, sir? If those boxes have been broken open once they've been broken open a dozen times. It's all very well saying 'Come unto Me', but you have to use your loaf, don't you? I don't know, I'm sure."

We were all standing there in the churchyard, in the long grass. A smell of fried fish blew across from a shop over the road and made me feel hungry.

"For all I know," Mr. Hanks went on, "you may be from *This Is Your Life*. They try all ways to get you, I'm told."

Toby made a sound like a snort. No one else said anything.

"Hasn't Mr. Benson left anyone in charge?" demanded Toby at last. "Who takes the services?"

"Different clergy, sir. Visiting. Mr. Benson arranged that

40

before he went off to Shanklin." He turned to Mrs. Rode. "Why don't you go and see the Abbey, madam? Now that is something to see."

"We-don't-want-to-see-the-Abbey—at least, that can wait," Toby said in his patient voice, which means that he is drawing near an explosion, "we want to see the Register of Marriages. This gentleman comes from the States, his great-great-great-grandfather was married in this village. I told you."

"Why not try Somerset House in London, sir?" Mr. Hanks demanded, turning to Mr. Rode.

"I have done so already. They were most courteous but their records only go back as far as 1837," said Mr. R.

"Come, Mr. Hanks," said Mrs. R. in a coaxing kind of voice, "I'm sure you don't really believe we're delinquents —why, Reverend Morgan Schrieber, our own vicar in Maine, would tell you we're regular church-goers, back home." She laughed her tinkling laugh.

"I'm only carrying out Mr. Benson's orders, sir."

But I could see that, for some reason, Mrs. Rode had convinced him we were all right. He shrugged his shoulders and turned away towards the church, and we followed him.

The little path he led us down went between more of this very very tall, very green grass until we came to a small old door in the wall of the church, at the side. I picked a piece of the grass and chewed it, in spite of Toby's frown. It's the kind of thing he hates me to do; he says it looks unsophisticated. But I was hungry.

"In here, please," said Mr. Hanks in a severe voice, opening the little door, "this here is the Vestry."

The entrance was so low that Toby and Mr. Rode had to stoop. It was just comfortably tall enough for me. Inside it was shiny brown wood and old stone and there was a smell of oil-firing and old books. Mr. Hank went across and opened a little cupboard with a key from a bunch in his pocket, and

41

took out a big old book bound in faded brown leather and laid it on a table.

"Goes back to seventeen fifty-one," he said, "belonged to the other church, what was burned down in 1815. Before the French Revolution, this one is. No telly in those days and who's to say they was any the worse for it? Let me, madam —it may be dusty. The last wedding here was in 1960."

He took a duster from a kind of little hole in the wall filled with all kinds of church junk, old crosses made of palm leaf and so forth and dusted the book.

We all bent over it as Mr. Rode began to turn the pages backwards in time, and we all watched him. I could read the dates—1860—1830—1792. The writing got paler, as time went on, a kind of dead-leaf colour the same as the cover of the book, and the writing more curvaceous. There was a faint perfume of mustiness.

"Ha!" said Mr. Rode suddenly, pointing, and we all crowded closer.

There it was, two names, and the date. "Maria Jane Wicks to Jabez Road, June 20, 1763."

"It's spelt differently," I said.

Mr. Rode was gloating over it—or I thought he must be. With his kind of face you can never tell. Toby frowned at me as I hid a yawn. If only we could go to lunch!

"Names often vary in their spelling in the course of time," Mr. Rode said, giving me his solemn smile, "especially if they are written by someone in a hurry where education is poor. Well, well. This is a great moment for me." Then he turned to the man Hanks.

"I should appreciate it if I might take a picture," he said, beginning to fuss with a tiny camera all over knobs that hung round his neck. Very expensive looking.

"Oh yes do, Clay. It will make a wunnerful first page for the book."

42

(They were making a photographic record of the ancestor-hunting.)

But Mr. Hanks was shaking his head.

"I doubt if you can do that, sir. Not without permission from Mr. Benson."

"But— —"

"And he'd have to get permission from the Parochial Church Council. You see this here is Church property."

"Oh for heaven's sake," said Toby, "can't you overlook it? We'll put a couple of quid in the Restoration Box."

"That's bribery," Mr. Hanks said, in a satisfied kind of voice.

But even while this was being said Mr. Rode had been adjusting his tiny camera like lightning, and just moving his thumb.

He caught my eye, and smiled, and Mr. Hanks started.

"You're a quick mover, sir," he said in a reproachful voice. "Well," he turned to me, "perhaps you'll bear me witness, miss, I tried to prevent it."

Anyone would think we had been forging the Crown Jewels.

"It's nothing to do with me," I said in a kind of mutter, because there's nothing I hate more than breaking the law. Toby says I am hopeless about this and have not a trace of aristocratic confidence. Well, why should I have? My father was a French journalist, not an exiled duke.

"Well, if that's all, I'll be off," said Mr. Hanks in a sarcastic voice, and off he stumped, standing aside in cross silence to let us file through the door, and then locking it up and trying the lock afterwards as if we were going to sneak back and steal something.

He also ignored the pound note Toby was trying to slip him which I think was noble of him as I'm sure vergers can't be paid much. He did not say good-morning to us and then he

43

went off to a door in a wall, over which a sad little house was looking.

"Now——" said Mr. Rode rubbing his hands, "Lunch."

I could see that Toby was pleased with how the morning had gone, because while we were eating a good lunch at a place with a French name and a licence which had set itself up outside Waltham Abbey to attract tourists, he drank more than usual.

He drinks very little, as a rule. He says he can't keep his eye in if he is half . . .—and then he uses a word which I will not write. But today he drank three glasses of wine.

The Rodes seemed to take it for granted there should be this quite expensive place near a noisy, not exclusive village like Waltham Abbey. But I thought it was sort of peculiar, the check tablecloths and wine, and the French advertisements on the walls, and then you looked outside and saw the low Epping hills and a discouraged sort of river winding along through shabby fields. It should have been roast beef and beer.

Well, after lunch I felt rather flat, like you do when someone's wedding is over. I think Toby did, too. He usually does unless he knows that something nice is going to happen almost at once.

But Mrs. Rode saved the day. She said, "Let's go and look at that wonderful old Abbey." I supposed that that was better than just going home.

So we piled into The Car again and drove the half-mile back to Waltham Abbey.

Now, as I have already said, I do not like churches. Or Abbeys or Cathedrals or any kind of large quiet religious place. And the day, beginning so brightly, had clouded over and we thought it might rain.

Inside the Abbey there was dusk, but it was a clear dusk, and through it the stained glass windows glowed, in shades

44

of sea green and a kind of light red which gave you a piercing feeling. It all smelt of very, very, very old stones, and there was no one about and you felt it had nothing to do with what was going on outside.

I also felt that everything I had done so far that day was wrong.

This is how old quiet large churches always make me feel, and if they make other people feel like that, too, you can't wonder, can you, that not many people go to them?

The roof was all painted with a crazy sort of—no, crazy is not the right word. It was complicatedly painted—no, and I don't mean that, either. The painting, the actual putting of the red and green and white on to the stone wasn't complicated, but the pattern was. Very unusual in a church, which usually has just wooden beams or a lot of dreamy angels.

"Why, they're the Signs of the Zodiac," exclaimed Mrs. Rode, who had bought a guidebook. "What a queer thing to put in a church. Downright Pagan."

That word again. Mem. the dictionary. But I knew about the Zodiac, because Mrs. Raven used to tell our fortunes, and I was able to explain to Mrs. Rode, while we stood craning our necks, about the Twins, and Aquarius and the others.

I could feel that Toby was pleased. Because, so far, I hadn't done much towards making the Rodes like me.

But I had really had enough of this old place, and I was relieved when we stepped outside.

Flatness was threatening again. The clouds were right down over the housetops, now. But still no rain.

"Well, sir — —" said Toby to Mr. Rode, "what do you feel like doing? Do you think we've pursued our enquiries far enough for to-day, or would you like to see if we can chase Jabez and Maria a little further?"

Mrs. Rode touched her husband's arm and murmured, "Don't forget to-night — —"

45

"Oh—yes—of course. No——" Mr. Rode said, "I think we've done enough for the first day. I think we'll go home. It is nearly a quarter of three." And he added, "I'm very well satisfied, Toby."

So we went. But imagine—that evening about five Mr. Rode telephoned us at that dreary flat to say they had tickets for *Sail Away*, and would we have dinner with them and go to see it afterwards.

Toby was radiant. He said they had obviously fallen for us in a big way. Perhaps they *were* our big chance.

And it was true. They were—are—kind. They couldn't be kinder. That's part of the trouble.

V

WE didn't go into Hertfordshire for the next few days after that because the Rodes had some American friends arriving in London and were sight-seeing with them. So we stayed at home. Not much though because we both adore the cinema and Toby had a lot of the money left that the Rodes had advanced him and we went to the cinema four times, in the most expensive seats.

Toby warned me, in case I should make a blunder, that he had told Mr. Rode, seemingly frankly, that we didn't live an ordinary young-married-couple life. He said he didn't want a regular job that he could get on in, and I didn't want a settled home. We liked to live adventurously, and take on queer kinds of jobs like this ancestor-hunting, while we were both young.

Of course this wasn't quite true. We don't really take on queer jobs as a regular thing. Toby isn't always perfectly truthful.

But neither am I and who on earth can be?

Toby said that Americans were used to the English being eccentric.

Guy had to have The Car, so we went to the cinema by taxi and back by one, too. Taxis are a thing we both adore. They are not a trouble like a car, with petrol and going wrong and repairs and things, and the drivers are so sweet.

Toby went straight through Oriel-man's shirts and started on his ties, and I hoped and trusted he might not come back from Algeria or the Congo or wherever it was.

One morning when Toby had gone to see Guy, I came back

from having my hair done and Miss de Havilland was talking on the stairs to another old thing.

This one was small, compared to tall old Miss de Havilland, and also elderly, and she looked poor, which was not a thing that Miss de H. and Mr. Pegram looked. I don't mean that they were smart, of course, but their clothes were awfully good, and well-kept. This one was an absolute bundle.

I said good morning and Miss de Havilland introduced me to the other one, who was a Mrs. Rawlings.

"How do you do. It is a pleasure to talk to anyone so young and pretty," said Mrs. Rawlings, which I felt was a good start. "We were just discussing these poor children who persecute us—yes, it is persecution. What they need, of course, is love."

"Stern love, like that of God," put in Miss de Havilland.

I do think older people are *extraordinary*.

"*I* love them," went on Mrs. Rawlings, opening her eyes very wide at me. They were like greengages. "I love them through my front door, which, as you may have noticed, dear child, has a broken panel. (Number nineteen. The new owners sent a man to break it in the small hours. But no matter.) I sit there, listening to their noise—which I must admit is exceedingly trying—and concentrate the Rays on them. If I had not done so, at the expense of some nervous energy I can ill afford, things might, who knows? have been worse. But of course when once the Rays do get through, they are *irresistible*."

"What rays?" I asked, thinking in a vague sort of way about science fiction.

"The Rays of love, of joy, of hope, of positive thinking," said Mrs. Rawlings. "They are there, always, for anyone to draw upon. But there, I am sure you think I am insane."

As she had exactly guessed my thoughts I felt a bit guilty. But she didn't seem to mind. She went on cheerfully—she

48

wasn't at all a dreary type—"No, far from that, I often think that I and others like me are the only sane people in an insane world. You will say that that is a *sign* of insanity."

"Rhoda, I cannot stay here any longer," said Miss de Havilland, beginning to move away. I did, too. Mrs. Rawlings took no notice beyond talking slightly louder and moving after us with a kind of delaying hand held out. "It is difficult to oppose that view. But I simply have to bear it," she went on.

She bowed her head and kept it like that for a bit. Her hat was like a perfectly round basin, faded to no colour at all, with a withered ribbon round it.

"And I can bear it," she said, popping up again, "because I am full of love. How could I bear these brutal attempts to get me out of my home, otherwise? And I have the Public Libary."

She tapped an old shopping bag, full of three absolutely enormous books. "Oh, how I praise the names of famous men who first thought of Public Libraries! So much pleasure, so *much* information, and all for a few decimal fractions on the rates. No, with the Rays, and reading, and full of love, I can joyfully run what is left of my race. And now I expect you would like to go about your own affairs. And I have to do my Pools. So farewell."

She nodded to us in a joyful kind of way and bundled off.

I glanced at Miss de Havilland. By this time we were climbing the stairs—slowly, because I remembered that her heart was bad. She looked at me seriously in return.

"You must not think," she said in a governessy kind of voice, stopping to rest, "that Mrs. Rawlings is slightly insane, or even an old fool. She is a clever woman, far cleverer than you or me. She holds several degrees and she has all those Pools at her finger tips. *I* never could understand them—(not that I have tried very hard. Tedious.) Her husband, who was devoted to her, was a classic scholar, famous in his day. That was forty years ago in another world. Would you like to come in for some coffee?"

Snowy appeared as she opened her front door, looking hatingly at us, as usual.

"Thank you very much, how kind of you." Toby had taught me to say this kind of thing.

She glanced at me approvingly as we went into the long room which served as living-room in all these flats.

The sunny morning shone on all kinds of antiques, a long shabby old mauvey-pink Persian carpet and a big varnished screen—from China, probably—all over lilies and dragons, and a white and crimson Paisley shawl draped over a couch.

Worth quite a lot, I should think.

The pictures on the walls were all religious—Our Lady, and Saint John, and the Holy Innocents. I already knew that Miss de Havilland was a Catholic and I didn't want her to find out that I had been baptised as one. She would probably fuss. So I only looked at the pictures while she was away making the coffee.

This was the first time I had been to coffee with her and as she was an old maid I expected her to be inquisitive about us —Toby's job, and whether I would have a baby soon, and so forth. But she didn't talk about us at all. She said straight out that she felt like chattering, this morning, and my part was to sit and listen.

Now I get all my ideas about rich and well-connected people from Toby who of course is mad about them, next to me, they are his favourite thing. But Miss de Havilland, though plainly a well-connected type, didn't talk at all as I had imagined those sort of people do.

Her voice was as soft as that powder of Helena Rubinstein's that is sifted through silk, yet clear, and with a pure kind of note. But she didn't mention a single title, or say anything in praise of where people lived (like *They had a mar-*

vellous castle in Scotland for example) or whether they had important jobs.

It was quite plain to me that she wasn't trying to show off.

She kept on using expressions that I didn't understand—"attached to the Embassy"—for instance. And mentioning people I'd never heard of—the Plesses—and "that tiresome boy, Carol—*she* was really rather charming".

I saved up these names to ask Toby knowing it would interest him, though I supposed of course they might all have died before his time—Miss de Havilland being ninety-one.

(Mr. Pegram told us. I am sure she never would have, though most old ladies like to boast when they get as old as that.)

Well the coffee-break passed quite cheerfully, and I am only mentioning it because this chapter is rather concerned with *old people*.

But you must not think I minded having them all round me, though they nearly all were old, in Rowland Mansions. The fact was, I rather liked having neighbours.

We had always had them at home, though they usually lived only in some house where we boarded. My mother was a friendly soul and interested in others. They were always interested in her too because she was married to a Frenchman and a journalist, which certainly is romantic.

I expect you are wondering why my parents never had a settled home. Well, as a family we all had this craze for the sun, which as you know of course we hardly ever get in the rainswept isle of England, and my father's idea was that we should have one really gorgeous holiday in the South of France every year, and save up to buy a little house there when he retired. But he never could save much because we were all three so fond of eating out and going to shows, and when he died there was next to no money and what there was went on his funeral and my mother's and that secretarial course for me. What was left I spent on my *trousseau*.

Chosen by Toby. Though I did let Mrs. Raven advise about two dresses, the only gaudy ones I have now, and I keep them for washing-up in.

You cannot wash up in black. You would look like a Cypriote.

VI

Two days droned past, with visits to the cinema and gossip with the local oldies and then the Rodes rang up and said, how about some more ancestor-hunting?

"We had a terrific bit of luck, you know, Idle, hitting straightaway on that old church," Toby said, as The Car went gliding down Finchley Road in the bright morning.

"It's practically the only one in Waltham Cross," I said, "I expect the Abbey has always reigned supreme, competition-wise." I was pleased with this expression. I got it off an advertisement and adopted it for my own use, as sounding sophisticated.

But Toby groaned.

"Do try to talk the Queen's English—as we're lucky enough to have the Queen," he said, "you're not to say that again."

Toby has deep loyalty and admiration for the Queen. He is absolutely the opposite in every way of an angry y.m.

Well, the Rodes came out, smiling and kind, as usual, and off we went.

As soon as we were well away, Toby said to Mr. Rode—

"If you approve, sir, my plan is this. I thought we would drive to Waltham Abbey again, and see if we can find anyone who remembers anyone living there named Rode."

Mr. Rode looked attentive but you can never tell what he is thinking.

"There may even be some people of that name living there. We could look up a local register of addresses," Toby went on.

"Or find someone *very* old, the oldest person in Waltham

53

Abbey," I put in, and Toby, though he hates having suggestions from other people, glanced approvingly at me.

"Yes, it's astonishing how far local memory and tradition goes back in some English villages. Until the war and the terrific increase in car-owning, life in these little places outside London had hardly moved since 1914. We'll find the local oldest inhabitant," he said, pleased.

What a ghastly task, I thought.

"Fine, fine," said Mr. Rode. "This is fun, isn't it, Marybelle?"

Mrs. Rode tinkled and beamed and nodded.

I wondered just how we were going to do it. Because you can't go round shouting at people, how old are you? (I once knew a boy who told me Russians always ask how old you are, at once, when they first meet you, but this wasn't Russia.) The last time we were in Waltham Abbey there were a lot of old men sitting on benches outside the Abbey so I supposed we'd have to go there again and ask one of them.

No old women, I had noticed. Too busy, I expect.

Suddenly I remembered my Aunt Edie.

I usually try to forget her because Toby gets so bored with absolutely ordinary cheerful people, and Aunt Edie is just like that.

She is a district nurse, retired because of a bad back, my mother's much elder sister and my only living relation except my father's brother in France. I hadn't seen much of her since my wedding, though I always send her a card at Christmas and also one with lilies on it at Easter asking how her back is because she is slightly religious.

But I will get on to her later.

The point is that she does this Meals-on-Wheels business for old people who are too feeble to go out for themselves, and if we could find a Meals-on-Wheels van or person in

54

Waltham Abbey, we could ask them the address of absolutely the very oldest person they called on.

I kept this good idea quiet, not wishing to introduce thoughts of Aunt Edie.

When we got to Waltham Abbey it looked as if it would rain any minute but—great luck and imagine—there opposite the very Abbey itself was a Meals-on-Wheels van. The driver was studying a noteook.

"I'll tell you what," I said quickly, waving my hands about as Toby encourages me to do when I get an idea because he says it looks pretty, "there's one of those Meals-on-Wheels vans. They deal with old people. I'll just leap across and ask the address of the oldest one she goes to, shall I?"

"Yes, do," said Toby. I could see he was annoyed because I had said leap. It is one of Mrs. Raven's words.

The one in the Meals-on-Wheels was elderly and all red and grey and teethy. But she was kind and terrifically interested in our ancestor-hunting, asking all kinds of questions, and staring across at The Car. I got the information I wanted and ran across the road back to the others.

"It's all right," I said. "Mrs. Sweeting. She's a hundred— imagine. She used to live in Waltham Abbey but a year ago she moved out to Datchet's Cross to be near her relations. She's quite hale and hearty and Miss Pickering says she has a splendid memory."

"Who in heck's Miss Pickering—oh, the character in the van—(how you do get on with people, don't you?)," muttered Toby, ignoring Miss P. who was smiling and waving, "and where's Datchet's Cross?" It was starting to rain.

He pulled out the large-scale map of Hertfordshire he had bought. The Rodes were leaning over from the back of the car to look.

" 'Tisn't marked," said Toby at last.

"It's between Bumbles Green and Didgemere, she said," I said.

The rain was starting to pour.

"This is fun!" suddenly said Mrs. Rode, dimplifying, and this cheered Toby up, in the middle of feeling, I am sure, it wasn't at all fun.

"It's absolutely *tiny*, she says," I said, turning to wave to Pickering, who was driving away, "it's a row of new bungalows, at the bottom of a hill with millions of nettles all round them. She said to look out for the nettles."

"Oh. Well, there seems to be a road direct to Bumbles Green——" and Toby started the car and we were off.

Heavens, it was coming down now. The big trees lashed about in the wind and the little houses and the daffodils and the fields of new green corn simply cowered under the rain. An April storm.

You can't call that part of the country between Essex and Hertfordshire really lonely but it looked lonely that morning. We only passed a few cars, with windscreen wipers working like mad. We also passed a board saying it was now Hertfordshire. The buds on the hedges were the most brilliant green in the streaming rain and birds kept on darting out of them and flying almost under the car. Once we all shouted at a gorgeous pheasant legging it across the road through the puddles and Toby had to brake quickly.

"There!" he said suddenly, as we approached a sign post. "Datchet's End—we must be near it."

"No, don't *whatever* you do go to Datchet's End," I said firmly. "Miss Pickering said it's miles from Datchet's Cross and has nothing to do with it."

"But it must have. It's the same name."

"They *aren't*, she said. She was *most earnest*. It would take you simply miles out of your way, she said."

"Oh. Well—upward and onward."

56

Mr. Rode entertained us with stories about places you couldn't find in Maine, U.S.A. I knew that Toby was feeling that places in a country that size had a right to be un-get-at-able, but places in a weeny county like Hertfordshire hadn't. He was getting hungry and cross.

But I think the Rodes were enjoying it. I am sure Mr. Rode was. Perhaps when you have all that money and everything mapped out and comfortable it makes a pleasant change to get practically lost on a wet morning in an out-of-date place like England.

We passed Bumbles Green, we passed Didgemere and still no sign of Datchet's Cross. Then Toby stopped a man plodding along under a sack. He was a surly man—I suppose because he had to walk while everyone else all round him had cars or at least a bicycle—and, as usual, the directions he gave were confusing.

(Though I never listen, myself, to directions. I am always too interested in looking at the person who is giving them.)

We wouldn't never get that thing down Farthing Hill, he said, which led to Datchet's Cross. Four miles back, it was. The signpost said Haymere but it led to Farthing Hill and down that to where we wanted. Then he stomped on in the rain.

When he heard we had to go back four miles Mr. Rode sat back and said "Whew!" and Toby was starting to look really sick but pulled himself together.

"Your system of mapping and naming over here seems very—individual," said Mr. Rode, not nastily. But I could see that Toby didn't like it. As I told you, he doesn't take criticisms of England.

Mrs. Rode just laughed. She really was a dear. But you know how men hate discomfort. Even my father wouldn't make jokes about it.

Toby says women have no proper feelings about discom-

57

fort, which is a serious thing which wears out your nerves and body and soul. He gets annoyed if I laugh when things go wrong.

I could see he was irritated again. The Car was going heave —whoosh—crash down Farthing Hill. It was a narrow steep lane streaming with water and the bushes on either side and overhead whipped against the sides with a scraping noise and we were jolted about as if on a rough sea. I held on to my hat to protect my head from bumping on the roof and Mrs. R. crossed both hands over her veil with the tiny velvet bows.

Mr. Rode kept on about the sack-man we had spoken to, saying he had quite a definite rural accent, and was it Essex or Hertfordshire, and were rural accents dying out in England under the influence of television? Toby answered intelligently—that is, he sounded as if he was listening—but I knew he was detesting it. In circumstances of discomfort he likes to concentrate utterly on getting out of them. Besides it was quite a dangerous lane, and it was Guy's car.

Well when we got to the bottom of the hill it was practically a swamp in a forest, surrounded by the stumps of trees with a muddy road full of puddles running away to nowhere, and a little hut and a lot of workmen's tools and things at the end of it. Evidently it was going through the forest and not finished yet and no workmen because of rain or something. Sitting alongside it was a row of bungalows, quite tidy, with clean curtains and television but looking naked and miserable, somehow, in the rain and the middle of the forest.

"This must be it," I said, "Mrs. Pickering said the road wasn't finished," and Mrs. Rode looked all round her and said again that this was *fun*. This time, Toby could not help giving her a hating look.

"It looks as if it never will be finished," he said. "Did your friend Pickering tell you which is Mrs. Sweeting's number?"

58

Jumpy, you see. And didn't like Pickering waving and smiling.

"Oh no, she just said everybody knows everybody else down here."

"I'll bet they do," poor Toby muttered. He loathes getting wet, and now he might have to.

(Writing getting smaller and smaller. Shall have to get more writing-pad from *somewhere*—oh goody, I have just remembered someone we stayed with gave me a five-year lock-up Diary which I never began and I brought it out here because I thought it might come in useful describing gorgeous days of sun-bathing, poor me. It has only three pages used up.)

"There's someone, in the nearest garden, darling, getting something off the line," I said.

"I'll just go and——" He was out of the car and sprinting along in the rain shouting "Hi—please——" before anyone could say anything.

Not that we seemed to want to. It was quiet and warm and sort-of cosy in the car, with the two flower-scents on Mrs. Rode and me smelling faintly and the Rodes looking kind.

"Miss Pickering will be interested to hear how we get on," I said.

"Did you exchange addresses? You weren't over there longer than a snap," Mr. Rode said, smiling.

"Well, kind-of. She said the Meals-on-Wheels Headquarters, Cheshunt, Herts, would always find her. That's the worst of me. I always get talking, if I'm not careful."

"Why should you be careful? We're here to talk to one another, surely?" said Mr. Rodes. And then he looked out of the window and said something about *love one another or die*. I couldn't quite hear. Mrs. Rode just smiled, and didn't say anything.

I wondered if they were religious? But I liked them, all the same.

59

As for being here to talk to one another, that wasn't Toby's idea at all. So I didn't say anything either, and then Toby came back.

"She lives in the end one. Believe me or not, it's called Blenheim. And the others are Chatsworth, Hatfield and so on. The rain's stopping." He opened the door of the car.

"That was her great-great-grand-daughter," he explained.

"Isn't she coming too?" someone asked.

"She has to attend to a baby," said Toby, in a disliking kind of voice.

"I hope we don't scare the old lady. Is she bed-ridden?" Mr. Rode asked as we picked our way between the puddles, through the thinning rain. Horrid though the country is I must admit it smelled good, and at the forest's edge I could see some primroses. And the nettles, warned of by Pickering.

"Oh no. The great-great-grand-daughter made rather a point of a hundred being no age nowadays. And she quite took the ancestor-hunting for granted. They get used to all kinds of situations, of course, if they have television."

Blenheim was a nice little house.

Of course I knew Toby was scorning it, because it was exactly like millions of other little houses, but I liked the white terylene curtains and the lawn in front with spring flowers and the front door painted mauve. I liked it better than Rowland Mansions, with that living-room that felt as if hundreds of men had sat up all night in it, plotting.

We did ring the bell, which had one of those lovely chimes, and then Toby noticed the door was ajar.

So Mrs Rode—as we decided in whispers—called in a kind voice—"Mrs. Sweeting? May we come in, please?" and there was a kind of faint squawk—good heavens what a word to spell but that was just what it was—from somewhere inside and in we went. Wiping our feet of course.

Everything was bright and new, with one of those flights

of china ducks I like flying up the modernly papered wall and a new carpet all over cheerful squiggles on a blue ground. It was stifling hot and smelt of warm oil.

"Come along in," called the voice that had squawked, louder now, "first door on left—if you're coming."

So Mrs. Rode opened the door and went into a hot, quiet room, all bright and new like the hall and full of house plants, and each wall done in a different paper. Very cheerful.

An old lady sat by the oil heater in the fireplace.

She *was* old; I had never seen anything so old that was still alive, though she was dressed in quite a modern way in a flowered dress with short skirts and her hair had been permed and rinsed blue. But over her shoulders she had a great woollen shawl, made of squares of different coloured wool sewn together, old-fashioned looking, and faded by washing, and somehow that suited her better than everything else in the room. It was a nice old face, what you could see for the wrinkles, solemn, but kind.

"Yes, sir. What is it, please?" she said in a faint, faint voice, to Toby, and went on almost at once, "if it's the Help Yourself Club I'm afraid I can't take out any tickets. I've only got my Pension and what my great-great-grandson allows me."

Her voice wasn't coarse or rough. It was what you might call refined and I remembered Miss Pickering had said that about eighty years ago Mrs. S. had been a maid, in a big mansion nearby.

"It's all right, Mrs. Sweeting, we've only come to pay you a little visit," Toby said in his gentlest tone—I knew that he was thinking how dreadful it must be to be so old—and then he went on to explain that this lady and gentleman were from America, just motoring round, and looking at England, and he explained how we had got her name and address.

"Miss Pickering's a very nice lady, only a bit inclined to

61

run on," Mrs. Sweeting said. "It's never having been married. They get like that, even gentry. Not that Miss Pickering is real gentry, of course," she added, as if she were talking to herself, "you aren't from the telly, are you?" Toby told her, kindly, that we weren't.

We were all sitting down, now, on the red leatherette chairs.

"Pat, that's my great-great-grand-daughter, she's got one. I go in there Thursday evenings. But mostly I go to bed at half-past four. Pat brings my tea at six and then I look at the paper a bit and doze off."

We all nodded in an admiring kind of way, and after Mr. Rode had said surely she didn't sleep alone in the house and she had said oh no Mr. and Mrs. Brewer came in at seven, they had a business in Hoddesdon and owned the house and Pat's husband, Wal, was very good he paid the rent of this room and the oil for the heater, Toby took matters firmly in hand and asked—

"Mrs. Sweeting, you have lived in the neighbourhood all your life, haven't you?"

"Yes. Waltham Cross and the Abbey and round there. Different places. There's some nice shops in Hoddesdon but aren't the prices terrible! Tenpence a pound for that Dutch butter or wherever it comes from—no, that was before the other war, the one they call the old Kaiser's war, I lost my son Harry in that war with the Dutch, the Boer War, that's it. Harry was my eldest. He was a good son."

We made sympathetic noises.

"It's all wars, isn't it?" said Mrs. Sweeting and Mr. Rode said in the voice that meant he was making a sad sort of joke, "You have a point there, madam."

"*I* don't know why all these foreigners can't realise that we manage things the best way for everybody," said Mrs. Sweeting, who was now looking quite lively.

"Well——" Mr. Rode was beginning still in his joke-voice, when I saw Mrs. Rode just put one finger in its pearly glove on his wrist, and he stopped.

"I wonder, Mrs. Sweeting, if you could kindly cast your memory back for us," said Toby.

"I've got a wonderful memory for my age. The young lady from the paper—*I've* never seen such a get-up but she was a nice young girl—she said I might be seventy, not a hundred. I had a telegram from the Queen. You think of that. Not but what I don't get very tired, sometimes. Pat, that's my great-great-grand-daughter, she says—'Oh, I'm fed up with you and your tiredness, you were born tired.' Hasn't much patience. Well, the young, they haven't. Life'll teach 'em."

"I was wondering," Toby said patiently, "whether you remember a family living in Waltham or Waltham Cross or anywhere in the district named *Rode*. R-O-D-E?"

After a little pause, Mrs. Sweeting slowly shook her head. "Can't say I do. It's a long time and Tom being a farm worker it wasn't like being in business or that, he'd be out working and I'd be at home with the children—didn't see much company."

"Perhaps—er—the Rodes kept a—were in business?"

"Give and take, I told her, that's what makes a happy marriage."

"R-O-A-D," put in Mr. R. "It could have been spelled either way." But Mrs. Sweeting only shook her head. She was beginning to look very tired.

"What d'you think of these teenagers?" she asked, trying to be sociable, poor old thing, "if you ask me what they need is a lot less money and a good smack on the bottom. And all this Bingo. I told the young lady. Trousers, well Pat wears trousers, but hair all over her face and dirty hands. *I* noticed. I'm not blind though I am a hundred. There's the telegram I had from the Queen. Wal had it framed for me."

It stood on a little table all by itself and we all got up to look at it. I was wishing we could give up, and leave her in peace.

"Never thought I'd live to such a great age," she was saying, rather tearfully now. "Never been beholden to anybody. 'In the sweat of thy brow', it says in the Bible. Worked until I was eighty, going out charing— —"

"Yes. Yes. Well, it's been a privilege to meet you, Mrs. Sweeting," said Mr. Rode, gently taking her tiny old purply hand, while Toby whispered to me, "I'm afraid it's hopeless." Mrs. Sweeting was sniffling now, quietly, into an old piece of rag and she was saying something about the days being so long and no one ever coming in to see her and Pat having no patience, and she wished God would send his angel for her.

"I'll stay for a bit," I whispered to Toby, and he nodded.

He and Mr. and Mrs. R. went quietly out and I heard them shut the front door. Through the thin curtain I saw them picking their way through the puddles to the car.

And the minute Mrs. Sweeting heard the front door click, she took away the bit of rag from her face, and looked up at me. She was not crying so much as I had thought.

"They gone?" she asked, and I nodded.

"I'll tell *you*," she said, "because you've got a sweet gypsy face. I like young girls. I was young once. I remember the Rodes all right. They were bad lots. Poaching, petty thieving, rick firing—and I remember them changing the name when poor Kate's husband died and she couldn't stand the talk and the wickedness any longer, and she moved with the children over to Ware."

"Changing their name?" I said, surprised. It was so hot, and silent, in the little room now that everyone else had gone, I felt somehow excited.

Mrs. Sweeting nodded.

"Changed it to Rode. All in the law. Got a lawyer to

64

arrange it. She was a sharp woman, Kate. Now mind you don't tell anyone, dear. Saint Paul tells us not to, and there's no sense in stirring it up fifty years after poor Kate's dead and gone. Least said, soonest mended. But we kept in touch, Kate and me."

"But what was their name, then? Wasn't it Rodes or R-O-A-D-S?"

"When I was a young girl," said Mrs. Sweeting, "working at Cross Manor in the kitchen, peeling the vegetables, they was called Roadknight."

"Roadknight," I repeated carefully, feeling still more excited, and she nodded.

"Know why? 'Cause one of them not so far back, my grandfather could remember people who'd known his son, had been a highwayman."

Then I nearly did burst with excitement.

"Truly, Mrs. Sweeting? You mean—holding up stage coaches and demanding the ladies' jewels and making them dance with him?"

"I don't know about all that. But there was wickedness, and no respectability. (Poor Kate. She had her troubles.) I used to hear my grandfather talk of Jabez Roadknight, the highwayman. (In the eighteen seventies, that would be). Bad blood in the family."

I could seen, now, that she was very tired. Her whole face looked different.

"But—just one more question, Mrs. Sweeting. How did the name change first of all to Roadknight? Because their name *was* R-O-A-D, to begin with."

"Kind of a nickname, Kate used to say. Knight of the road, see. A highwayman. Didn't you ever hear them called that? When this here Jabez took to a life of crime, that's what they called all the rest of the family. Roadknights. Kate, she just changed it back again, only spelt different."

Well! Here was a thing.

"Thank you for telling me, Mrs. Sweeting," I said.

She put up her hands and pulled my face down and just lightly kissed my cheek.

"God bless you, my deary," she said.

VII

WELL, that was nice of her, but I hate touching old people, and you are not often touched by someone aged a hundred.

So the minute I got outside the house I ran across into the forest and pulled up some primroses and put them against my sweet gypsy face, and was enjoying the feel of them when I heard Toby calling rather crossly.

"Nancy! Buck up! We're all starving."

So I went back to The Car and Mrs. Rode admired the primroses and we spent the next twenty minutes getting out of Datchet's Cross and up that hill, and telling each other it was a pity we couldn't get anything out of old Mrs. Sweeting. Mrs. Rode asked me if she was still crying when I left and I said Oh no, she had cheered up a bit.

I was so excited about the highwayman and longing to tell Toby that I was quite glad when they started arranging about lunch, and I could sit back and think.

After a little while, I wondered if I would tell Toby, after all. Because, you see, he might take it in a funny way. I will try to explain.

Toby doesn't have the same ideas about right and wrong as most people have. Though I don't like religion, I am used to people going to Mass, and the idea of sin and so forth. I suppose I am a lapsed R.C., really. But Toby simply believes you can do whatever is most useful for you, and it doesn't matter.

Suppose I told him about the highwayman and he kind-of *held it over* the Rodes, even asking for money to keep it quiet?

You mustn't think that I don't trust Toby. I do, now, after

all that has happened. Truly I don't think we have any secrets from each other—now. But in those days, you see, I had only been married to him for about six months and I was so much in love with him that I never thought, do I know him really well? I only adored him, and everything he did had up till then been all right with me. (Come to that, it still is.) But I was already beginning to get slight uncomfortable feelings from time to time about some of the things he did and said. Oriel-man's shirts, for instance.

And although of course no one believes in Hell nowadays you don't want anyone to go there.

And even if he told the Rodes straight out, without asking for money to keep it dark, they mightn't like it at all. Perhaps all their fortune was founded on Jabez's *ill-gotten gains*. Who could know?

So I decided to say nothing. And imagine, the Rodes suggested lunch at the Berkeley to make up for a disappointing morning and though not particularly smart there it was interestingly formal. In the afternoon we just parted to change our clothes and rest, and in the evening, imagine, they took us to see *Blitz!* Supper afterwards.

That is the kind of life I like.

Up till now, I had found that the more you get into the habit of keeping secrets, the easier it gets. Like every time you think, no I won't, when you want another sweet. I never really wanted, after a few days, to tell my husband about old Roadknight. I just took keeping it dark for granted. Then things began to happen which caused my mind to change about secrets and mysteries and keeping them.

Things went on as usual. We didn't see much of Guy—at least, I didn't—because he got himself a new job quite easily of course with another firm, not driving for the moment because he had hurt his wrist slightly but advising and overlooking—I don't know. Anyway, he was busy, and so long as I didn't have to have him around, taking up Toby's attention and staring at me, I didn't care what he did.

The children went on firing peas at old Miss de Havilland, and shouting at Mr. Pegram, and Mrs. Rawlings went on being cheerful and getting in touch with those dotty Rays—and doing her Pools.

You would think Toby would be just the kind of person who would do the Pools, wouldn't you? because of wanting real money.

He would scorn to do them. He scorns *them*. Aunt Edie always does them, and so do all kinds of people. I could never make them out.

The Rodes were doing a little sight-seeing on their own, and it wasn't until nearly a week after we had interviewed Mrs. Sweeting that they rang us up.

We had seen *La Dolce Vita* and *Last Year at Marienbad* and *Road to Hong-Kong*—which last was dreamy and Toby hated it but went for my sake.

Now the Rodes said, could Toby take them down on a little excursion to see his aunt's place, Abbotstower?

I like to look at Toby nearly all the time, and I was doing so when this was suggested—I was sitting near the telephone and could hear plainly—and I saw him look doubtfully. But he said at once that he'd be delighted. Then I heard Mr. Rode say:

"The friends we've been staying with have met your aunt. George and Ida Winkler. They have a lovely home in Wiltshire, bought an old castle and made it over."

"Oh—er—yes?" said Toby, now looking in a way which it is difficult to make you see. Sick is the nearest word I can find, and I wondered why he was looking like that, over this perfectly ordinary remark?

"Lovely," repeated Mr. Rode. "There was some local flower-show last year and they met her there."

"She isn't often over in England. She certainly isn't at the moment, I'm afraid, I heard from her last week. She's at her villa, up at the back of Mentone. But of course I'll be delighted to take you, sir. What day would you like to go?" (I didn't remember seeing any letter or card. But Toby does have secrets.)

Toby was cross and moody all the rest of that day in a funny sort of way, but in the evening Guy rang up and said could he go out with him, and he went.

I spent the evening with old Mrs. Rawlings and very peculiar it was in her flat, all dust and enormous old books, and those Rays coming into the conversation every now and again as if she'd met them on holiday at Bournemouth. But she was nice. We had a jug of hot chocolate, and dripping toast.

The next day was beautiful, really warm, with all the trees that fresh light green which only comes in the month of May, and we soon got out of London, and all the may trees were in flower.

Toby took us a very roundabout way, to use the quiet roads and lanes shown him by Guy in their youthful motoring long ago, and just by Sutton there were hundreds of these may trees all covered in soft white and pink blossom. And the grass! So green. I wouldn't like to live in the country, as I'm always saying, but it certainly was dreamy.

We had taken a picnic with us, with wine, and we ate it under a may tree and Toby sang songs he had made up. He has a darling voice, my Toby. When he sings it is as if he were kissing me. He seemed to have got out of his queer mood.

I'm sure the Rodes enjoyed it, too.

Essex is a large county, with a lot of sky over it, and puzzly little lanes going off to unknown places, and almost every

70

house has a television aerial on the roof. We drove on and on, cheerfully, and there at last across quite a wild, though not lonely, bit of flat land was the sea, blue and rippling in the sun.

Now the sea I do like, especially when there is a pier with entertainments and Dodg'ems and stock-cars.

But here there were only flat meadows of marshy grass, with a wide slow river wandering through them beside sheets and sheets of gold flowers. There was an embankment shutting these fields off from the sea. The air smelt salty and clean.

"Great God," said Toby, as we drove into Helsea, which is the village for Abbotstower. "I do wish, sir, it was possible to show you just one English village that hasn't been spoilt."

"I can see what it used to be," said Mr. Rode, "and you know in most of our villages, except for those in New England, and one or two in Virginia, there's nothing like *that*," and he nodded towards the square tower of the old church, looking down on the little whitey grey houses.

"Saint Helga's," said Toby, "founded by a pious nun in 970. She was killed by the Vikings."

Mrs. Rode said, was that so, and Toby explained that all this coast for years and years had had Vikings coming down on it, in great ships with beaky birds on their fronts, doing dreadful tortures to the inhabitants and demanding ransoms. Mrs. Rode said she could just imagine it all.

Sometimes, I knew, Toby read about the places we were going to take the Rodes to, with guidebooks and maps, because I had seen him and we had laughed about it, but here I knew that he knew it all by heart. Because he loves this place and Abbotstower.

Of course it was the first time I had seen it and I didn't see how the village was spoiled, unless you don't like shops selling souvenirs, which I do. It did smell a bit of fried fish but not very much because as it was only May there weren't many tourists. The few that were there were wandering

71

about, staring into the shops. I wouldn't have minded doing that myself, but as we walked up towards Abbotstower I quite forgot about everything else.

The Keep stood up against the clear, very blue sky, looking strong and somehow gay. The two towers had an archway in the middle and they were inlaid with black and white stones—flints, Toby said—with slender bands of pure white stone going across, and there were those castle-y-looking finishes to each tower, up and down, up and down, also in black and white. It looked definitely un-dusty and clean. Washed by the sea wind and the unsmoky rain, I suppose.

You would be sure, with those frightful Vikings always threatening the poor souls living here, that they would build a grim, frowning, scarey castle out of huge lumps of granite or something to frighten them off, wouldn't yau? And you would be dead wrong, because what those characters did was just to have a couple of thousand waggon-loads of flints brought up from the beach a mile away and build up a castle as cheerful as some kid's toy fort.

You couldn't help respecting them. The sight of it made me want to call out "Good for you!"

Inside the archway you paid a shilling for a ticket to a woman in a white nylon coat and went on into the gardens. These, and the Keep were now owned by a sort of Body, but were open to the public and the money went to the upkeep of the ancient place. Lady South, or Aunt Hermy as I suppose I should call her, also let the public into her Keep, at half-a-crown a time, and *that* went to what Toby called one of her pet charities. I thought it a bit expensive.

"Tickets for the Keep?" said the woman to Toby, who always paid our smaller expenses on these expeditions.

"Er—yes, please. As a matter of fact——" Then Toby seemed to change his mind and bought the tickets without another word. "She's new since I was here last," he said to the

Rodes. "Old Mrs. Crossley has left. There wasn't much point in saying who I am."

The gardens really were beautiful, with the largest widest smoothest lawns I have ever seen and great old trees standing solemnly about them in early leaf. Like ancient giants with fresh young robes.

(It was all very well for The Spider to tell us to keep off descriptions whenever possible, because we couldn't do them and usually they set her teeth on edge, but sometimes you have what seems to you the right idea.

And she was there to teach us how to do them, not to have her teeth set on edge. I think they were dentures anyway, so how could they be? That was *inaccuracy*.)

There weren't many people about, a few families with children and pairs and pairs—quite six pairs—of those elderly ladies you see everywhere who go away together and have a nice peaceful time doing things they both enjoy. Like looking at flowers, and then having a cup of tea, and saying it will be nice to get home.

I hope I die before I get elderly.

(I have just remembered the name of the Body that owned the grounds. It was the National Trust.)

Toby showed us a wide thick knotted-up fig-vine, and a dragon carved in stone climbing over the door. He used to steal the figs when he was a little boy, and the scales on the dragon's rather fat legs used to frighten him terribly.

There was a smaller garden, too, with dark green ancient trees cut cleverly into the shape of birds and animals, and he said these used to remind him of the beasts in his Noah's Ark. He was full of high and good spirits, that day.

I noticed the people in the gardens, though, because I like people much better than things, and there was this little woman in a shabby purple tweed suit.

No hat, and hair that had been beautifully cut. I just

noticed her because of this cut. It must have cost a lot, but her hands were grubby, as if she had been gardening. She had a divine golden charm bracelet, the like of which I had never seen.

She rather clung to us. Well, one or two other people did, I suppose because they noticed Toby standing in front of things and telling us about them, as if he knew. There was no guide provided for Abbotstower, which was half a private home anyway.

A stout woman and her husband and two little boys clung to us and a schoolmaster-y sort of man and this little woman. She had a pale face and light grey eyes, long in shape, and she looked a little amused. Not a kind face. I should think it could look cruel, in a laughing way.

She rather flitted about, picking off dead leaves in an absent-minded way, some people can't help tidying up wherever they go, though I am far from like that myself, but every time she came back to our little crowd.

Well, when we came to go into the Keep, the woman in the white nylon coat came up to take our tickets and lead us through. We were all there by this time—our party, the pairs of elderly ladies in their light spring coats and sandally shoes, the stout woman and her family, and the little woman with the hair cut.

My goodness, the drawing-room of that Keep was luxurious. The walls were thick stone, of course, but that only made it look more fashionable, as stone walls are right in again, and on the stone floor there was a huge long delicate carpet in shades of palest orange and rose. Chinese, Toby said. Right down that great room.

All the furniture was antique, immaculately polished, and there were some Chinese gods and horses in pale colours sitting in little caves in the walls, and hundreds and hundreds of spring flowers in bowls. It was so quiet that you wanted to

74

tip-toe. "Let to a Danish gentleman," said the woman who was conducting us, "the owner lives abroad." She was the reserved type, that woman. I think she didn't like us being there. I saw her just glance at the woman with the hair cut. Perhaps—it was a disturbing thought—*she* was a friend of Aunt Hermy?

We only caught a glimpse of the bedroom, which had a white-covered bed with one of those newly fashionable brass frames, and a soft old turquoise carpet, because the woman whisked the door shut, but we saw the modern kitchen made in a little kind of monk's-cell, and there was a bathroom the other side, the woman said crossly in reply to an almost whisper from the stout woman's husband. One of the elderly ladies got up courage to ask where the Danish gentleman was?

"Out sailing. Mr. Gustaffson is very fond of sailing," said white-coat in a crushing voice.

Those Vikings were Danes, Toby had said. I wondered how Mr. G. felt, living in luxury in a Keep so often burnt down by his fellow countrymen, and sailing peacefully round this coast where they used to raid? I don't suppose he thought of it.

There is always *someone* upsetting things for ordinary people, isn't there?

Going back through the drawing-room the afternoon sun-light poured through a slit of a window on to a big, long couch covered tightly in orange satin, making it beautifully glow.

"Ah," said Toby, stopping in front of it, "that's an old friend." Rather to his irritation, I could see, everyone else stopped too. (Like an old song of Aunt Edie's *When father turns, we all turn.*) "It used to be in front of the fire in the winter, when I was a little boy, and covered in a kind of flowery stuff. I used to curl up on it and go to sleep."

"You're quite at home here, then," said the stout lady, not

75

in a pleasant voice, and everybody was looking interested. I looked at the woman with the hair cut. Her long eyes were almost hidden in a smile that made her seem like a cat.

Toby muttered and smiled and somehow got us out into the open air again. He gave old nylon-coat a large tip and she took it as if it were her right.

We had certainly had a happy time and I am sure the Rodes were pleased. Toby seemed still in high spirits, though I thought nervous, too, in some way.

Well, by this time it was four o'clock and he said that we had better get started on our homeward way perhaps, as, though he did know the bye-ways and lanes, it would be impossible to avoid the traffic crush altogether if we stayed much later. So we walked towards The Car parked outside the gates.

And just then someone called "Hi!"

We all turned, and there was the little woman with the hair-cut, coming out from under the archway with the dragon curling over it.

"You—just a moment," she said, singling out Toby, still cattily smiling.

"It's all right—you go on," he said quickly, and though I was rather surprised, we went. "Maybe she wants to know something special about the place, and overheard Toby saying he knows it well," Mrs. Rode said, and she slipped her arm through mine, which surprised me again. But I didn't mind.

Toby must have stayed quite ten minutes with the little woman, and we were all sitting in The Car when he came back. He was smiling.

"What did she want?" I asked.

"She'd lost a brooch and wanted to know if I'd seen it."

"Oh? What kind?"

"Diamond, she said." Toby got in beside Mr. Rode.

"I'm not surprised," Mrs. Rode and I said together and I

76

added, "Surprised it was diamonds. Did you notice her hair cut?"

"I didn't notice anything. I was wondering why she picked on me," said Toby. *I* noticed now how pale he was, almost green.

"Maybe she saw you were the only young male in sight," Mrs. Rode said in a demure voice and I could see that Toby liked this, and we all laughed. You laugh easily when you have had a good day.

"Oh, she was a lady," Toby said quickly, "but lonely, perhaps."

He started the car, and I knew that he meant the little woman had picked on him to ask because he is—was—a gentleman.

I don't know what the Rodes knew or felt. But on the way home Toby gradually became unusually quiet, and when we dropped them at the crumbling old Chandos, and Mr. Rode made the usual suggestion that we should meet later and go to a cinema, I think Toby was going to refuse.

But of course I sailed in and said it would be utter heaven and made all the arrangements, and we went to *Only Two Can Play*. I quite enjoyed it only I really prefer the French film comedians.

When we got into that place—(somehow, in spite of it being our first real kind of home, I couldn't think of it as such) I was so sleepy I went to bed at once. Toby actually said he would sit up a bit. He absolutely never does.

"Do you feel all right, darling?" I said.

"Perfectly. Don't fuss."

"Would you like a drink?" One blessing of the Rodes' twenty guineas was that now we could always have lashings of the stuff.

"No. No thank you. You run off into bed. I'm just going to have a word with Guy."

77

Oh, if it was Guy, of course. I felt jealous and inclined to *bouderie*, so I dropped a kiss on the back of his neck where he sat forward broodingly in one of Oriel-man's chairs, and floated off.

I heard them talking away for ages but couldn't make out a word Toby was saying. Not that I was really *trying* to. But whatever he was saying to Guy didn't seem to have done him any good, because when I woke up for a moment when he did come to bed, he was standing in his shirt-sleeves, looking down at me with the strangest expression, while he slowly unknotted his tie.

"Hullo——" I said only half awake.

"Hullo, my heart's nuisance. Go to sleep again."

"Are you coming to bed now?"

"What do you think I'm doing, Intelligence?"

But I couldn't go to sleep again at once. I lay awake for a little while, wondering, though I didn't say anything more. Because his expression has been sorrowful, and kind of ashamed.

VIII

WELL, from now on Toby changed.

In all kinds of little ways, not big ones. He was exactly the same to me, thank goodness, sweet and teasing. But he brooded, and sometimes I would catch him looking at me when he thought I didn't notice with that same odd expression.

Also, he suddenly started avoiding Mr. Pegram, whom he used rather to like. I never asked him what was the matter. I thought it wiser not.

Some girls pretend to have a Spanish or Italian grandmother. Because they think it makes them more romantic. There were at least three at school who did, and I was pretty certain it wasn't true. But I really did have a French father, and only a short time ago, and I believe that has made me more wise about handling a husband than most girls.

You see, Frenchwomen are simply born more feminine than Englishwomen and also they don't have this unnatural business at school of keeping a stiff lip and loyalty to the community and all that sort of nonsense. They are much more free to be proper women—afraid of loud bangs, and ready to forgive people, and that kind of thing.

I really believe the instinct of my Frenchwomen ancestors helped me from time to time with Toby. I strongly felt, now, that it would be most unwise to ask him what was the matter.

Though certainly something was.

Well, now, as well as all this slight but definite change in Toby, something simply ghastly and unbelievable happened to me.

79

No doubt you will think it was starting a baby—and when I think of Mary James's baby, the one I mentioned, few things could be more ghastly for someone who likes their sleep as much as I do—but you would be wrong. I suppose that God knew quite well that with these feelings I should not make an excellent mother, and so He did not over-ride our plans, but let us get on with it, deciding to pull us up short in another way.

I would not say so to Toby, even now, but though I don't like religion it is my absolute firm belief that *you cannot go one better than God.*

Though it doesn't worry me much as I am always interested in what is going to happen next.

Well, one day towards the end of May I was window-shopping in Oxford Street.

In fact I am never supposed to be there because Toby says Oxford Street is the ultimate end and its wares will corrupt the taste he has so carefully put into me about clothes, but the truth is that I like Oxford Street. There is so much to look at, and so cheap! I adore a bargain.

Toby likes me to window-shop in Knightsbridge, or those little streets all spread out behind Bond Street, with little expensive salad-y places where the debs and models go for lunch.

It's true I wasn't actually in the forbidden area but looking in a dress-shop window in South Moulton Street at the fatal moment.

I say *fatal* because nothing has been the same afterwards—except loving Toby. And the loving T. is in a different way.

I was looking at this yellow dress with the embroidery, dressed in black as usual, black terylene, and carrying my hat, which Toby will allow, and enjoying the sun blazing on my shoulders through the terylene, when a voice said—
".Hullo—how are they all at The Moorings?"

"Oh hullo Guy," I said, turning round, not pleased, and ignoring that silly joke. And I added "Have you been to a wedding?" because he was elegantly dressed in dark clothes, with a bowler, and a red carnation in his buttonhole.

"Wedding? Good Lord no. Lunching with a client." Then we didn't say anything for a moment. The sun shone down burningly on us, and the crowds hurried past over the warm stone pavements. London hummed and dazzled and roared joyfully in the May heat, and Guy looked at me. Oh, I can remember it all so well. Angelic London.

"Where's Toby?" Guy said next.

"Gone down to see that old man again—Mr. St. Merryn."

"Ah yes. The one who didn't like you. An old friend," Guy said. "Let's walk on, shall we?"

I didn't want to, but how could I say no, we won't? Besides, I set out to write the truth and I must now confess that I liked walking down that smart little street, wearing floaty black, with a man so well-dressed as Guy. What woman wouldn't. (Mrs. Rawlings, for one. She would sooner walk with those Rays—if they can walk.)

"How do you mean—an old friend?" I asked, as we walked on, "we only met him at a party some months ago."

Guy looked mysterious and signalled to a cruising taxi, which swerved to the pavement.

"*You* did, darling Nancy. Toby's known him—but never mind. Jump in," and he held open the door.

"Where are we going?" I got in, because it would have been rude and silly to make a fuss. Also, as I have said, I adore taxis.

One of the things I disliked most about Toby being such friends with Guy was all the secrets they had. Now there was seemingly one about this old man. But I said not a word. This can be a cause of strength to a wife—or to anybody, actually. I stared straight in front of me.

"Oh, this is just to get you out of the forbidden zone. Naughty Nancy—window-shopping in Oxford Street."

"It wasn't Oxford Street, it was South Moulton Street."

"Near enough. Toby would lecture you. We'll have tea at that picture place."

"What picture place?" I thought he meant some cinema.

"On the Embankment—the Tate, yes, that's it, the Tate. It's fairly quiet there."

Why did he want it to be quiet? I wondered. I am not fond of quiet places, unless you want to go to sleep.

I looked at him, in a casual way, and saw that his face appeared different.

This sounds peculiar. I don't mean that it didn't look like Guy. But it was kind-of agitated underneath itself, if you know what I mean. Like someone bottling down their feelings. I put the remark about old Mr. St. Merryn out of my mind. No doubt there was no harm in it, except a wish to tease me. All the same, I began to feel slightly uneasy.

"And where are the Rodes to-day?" he said next, as if trying to be pleasant.

"They've gone to sight-see at Wilton House, with some American friends. Mr. Rode likes to drive himself, sometimes. He hires a car."

"Don't you ever let that rebellious Colonial drive My Wife," Guy said.

"Oh Toby never would," I assured him, "I don't know how he would get out of it if Mr. Rode actually asked him if he could. But Toby would manage somehow."

"Yes, old Toby is highly ingenious."

You know, I didn't like the tone of that remark. *It ain't exactly what 'e says, it's the nasty way 'e ses it*, which is the title of another of those ancient songs known by my Aunt Edie, and it exactly expresses what I felt about Guy's tone.

The taxi stopped at last on the Embankment, and I turned

to look at the river gliding past, bright silver in the afternoon light, but Guy seized my arm and kind-of rushed me up the steps and past some awful bluey-purple paintings of clowns, at least I think that's what they were meant to be and down into the basement.

"Come along, you aren't the kind of girl that wants to look at those . . ." he muttered.

"Rouault. Who was he?" I said, not really wanting to look at the miserable-faced clowns but thinking I had better delay things a bit.

"Oh some Frenchman. They're all Frenchmen nowadays. Why anyone wants anyone but Gainsborough and Morland, and that other chap, Stubbs, is it? paints horses—I can't think. Now you've got me talking about *paintings* . . . Come along."

"I wouldn't mind looking at them," I said, still delaying.

"Oh darling Nancy, do come *along*," he said in such a voice that I stared at him. His eyes looked as if he had been drinking. I began to feel really alarmed. And down we went.

The tea room at that place is exactly what I like, long and cool with lovely flowing pictures of woods and castles and coaches and lovers all along the walls. There weren't many people there, and the brilliant light of the distant river shone in and made the tablecloths look very white. *Tea*, I thought, heavenly.

But he steered me into the darkest corner and sat me down at a table for two with my back to the wall and when the waitress came up he said in a distracted kind of voice, "Oh, toast. Lots of toast, please, and china tea."

Now if there is one drink I do hate it is that watery china stuff and Toby has tried in vain to make me drink it. So I said, quite loudly and firmly, "*I don't like China tea.*"

And he took absolutely no notice.

I don't think he even heard. He was staring down at the tablecloth, with a troubled expression.

83

It was at this exact moment that my French ancestresses seemed to say clearly to me, *Now, Nancy Régine, the one thing you must not do is to get in a tizz.*

I don't mean that they would have said a tizz, they would probably have said something in French. But I felt they were dead right.

"Shall I pour out?" I said in a cool sort of voice as the waitress put down in front of us a pot and then a great mound of goosome buttery toast.

At least, I thought, I shall be able to keep my strength up, whatever happens. Goody for that.

He nodded, without looking up. Very strange.

So I began to pour out the weak, weary Chinese drip, keeping my eyes fixed firmly upon my job, and at that very instant Guy muttered something.

"What?" I said—Toby having told me that this is not really rude.

"It's all so damned awkward."

"What is?" I asked, taking a piece of toast.

"My—well—darling Nancy—the fact is——"

Silently I passed him the toast, which was hot and delicious, and he impatiently waved it away, causing me to think, good, all the more for me. I had to get what comfort I could.

I was getting irritated by the extraordinary way he was carrying on.

"I love you," he said, suddenly looking straight at me.

Happily I was not drinking the insipid Oriental brew (I think that is a good way of describing China tea, don't you?) at that moment, or I would surely have choked.

As it was, I sat absolutely dead still and quiet, with my mouth full of hot toast, and open, I'm afraid, and my cup kind-of suspended in my hand, just staring at him.

I felt as if the room had turned upside down and every-

84

thing was hanging like flies from the ceiling. Then I felt I absolutely could not have heard properly.

"What?" I said, beginning to chew again.

"Do you mean to tell me you had no idea?"

"Of course I hadn't. How could I have?" I said, hanging on desperately to the ancestresses. "Besides, I'm sure you aren't." It was what I honestly felt. In *love* with me? *Guy?*

"Oh yes I am, worse luck. From the first time I saw you (at Richmond. Remember? You had on a pink dress, it was before old Toby got to work on you.)"

"I thought you were going steady with that Lady Vanessa someone," I said, having seen the papers and heard gossip.

"Steady! No, that's—no, I am not. It's you," Guy said.

"Then I suppose it's one of your stupid jokes. Like The Moorings." I was beginning to feel rather desperate.

"Damn The Moorings . . . I've tried, I have tried, I swear it. Do you suppose I *enjoy* it? Toby's my friend . . . it's all so *awkward*."

"If you are speaking the truth it certainly is," I said, trying to behave normally.

After all, I was a married woman. This should have protected me from such extraordinary remarks. I should have loved some more toast but thought the situation was now so serious that I had better not take a piece. It was agony, though, seeing it get cool.

"If!" He made a despairing kind of face. "If you only knew. Darling Nancy, I've been off my driving for months. I can't sleep. I can't eat. It's absolute hell." He stared at me, in a piteous kind of way.

"Well do have some toast now, Guy," I said, the ancestresses advising me to use a motherly voice, "it's a pity to let it get cold."

I pushed the dish towards him, in a kindly way, and to my great surprise he laughed and took a piece.

85

"How can you wonder I love you, when you do things like that?" he said.

You will be surprised, I expect, to hear that I didn't feel angry with Guy for being in this state. In fact, I felt that I was liking him a very little, for the first time in my life. I took some toast as well, and drank some more horrid tea.

I felt slightly less stunned now, and was thinking out how to deal with him. I thought it would certainly be best to let him do most of the talking, especially as I didn't yet know what to say. But, now, I did *believe* him.

For some moments we munched in a tense kind of silence.

Then he bolted his mouthful and said quickly, not looking at me.

"You see, I was kind of hoping you'd come away with me."

I was stunned all over again. Before I could stop myself I said "*What?*"

"Nancy, if you keep on saying what I'll—I'll—Yes, I was hoping you would. Old Toby—we needn't hurt old Toby. That's the last thing I'd want to do."

"Nothing is going to happen, in that way, to hurt him," I said in a calm voice, stunned, but being inspired like mad now by the ancestresses. "Absolutely not."

We looked at each other. Guy's eyes, you know, were exactly the colour of that very good dark sherry.

"Quite sure, Nancy?" he said at last.

"I am very sure," I said, getting better and better at it and thinking it best not to sound heatedly certain, "and I am sorry, but you must try to get over your feelings."

My own feelings were now angry. After all, it was rather impertinent of him to kind-of hope, wasn't it? Wives don't usually go away with other men, especially when they have been married for only six months. I like being a wife, and I don't think of it as anything but my permanent state.

"You're very cruel," he said at last, in a silly kind of voice, "and you don't know anything—you're just so young it isn't true."

"I am young," I said, now wanting to hurt him, "but I belong to Toby and I like it and I don't want anyone else. Ever." I drank some tea, looking quietly out of the window.

He didn't say anything for some time. He sat back in his chair, staring at the toast plate. Then he look up, with an expression on his face I had never seen there before. He looked jeering, and cruel.

"You don't know much about Toby, do you?" he began, and then he stopped, and the expression went away, and he smiled at me, and got up from the table.

"All right, darling Nancy, loyal little wife, but you don't know yourself either, I think. I shan't give up hope. I haven't been watching you for six months for nothing." He caught the waitress's eye and beckoned her. "I say, are you going to mention this to old Toby?" He sounded quite casual.

The coolness of it, the real wickedness! When Toby was his best friend.

I just didn't say anything. I walked away to the cloakroom, which is very nice at the Tate Gallery as it often is at museums and such places, all cool and marbley and spacious.

I stayed there repairing my face and so forth, not thinking of anything but that, and now somewhat stunned again, and hoping that when I came out he would have gone.

But no, blow me down as Toby would say, there he was at the foot of the stairs, waiting.

"Will you tell him?" he said, as we walked up the stairs.

"You must wait and see," I said calmly, "if I do tell him, you will know, because he won't want to be friends with you any more."

"Well I hope you won't because I wouldn't like to hurt old Toby," Guy said, in a sentimental sort of voice.

In books I have sometimes read that people were speechless. I was now. I walked down those wide steps, out on to the Embankment. The silver river was running fast with the turning tide, away towards the sea, and in spite of the bright afternoon I felt troubled. I do like everything to be easy and simple, and I foresaw fearful puzzles lying ahead.

"Can I drop you anywhere?" he said.

"No thank you. I shall take a taxi," I said, in a cold sort of voice feeling that I deserved and needed this treat.

"Good-bye then, darling Nancy. Remember me."

He turned away, but just as he came to the corner, he turned round and walked right up to me again and said, looking down at me and laughing all over his face, "I say, what *would* they say at The Moorings?"

It was the last straw and I turned my back.

IX

Oh, how on that taxi ride home did I wish I had someone to talk to! I am not a natural bottler-up, really, though often I make myself bottle, out of my French wisdom, and now there was simply no-one.

Again and again I longed to tell Toby, but I knew that that was impossible.

I knew it right away. Because Guy was his best friend, and he would be livid, and dreadfully hurt. I even thought that he might not believe me. He did suspect, I sometimes felt, that I was jealous of him being such friends with Guy and having secrets with him, and silly jokes which I didn't find so funny, and he might think that I had made up this story, to try and end their friendship.

You see, I felt so stunned. And all the time I was wondering whether it was another of Guy's jokes, and thinking how embarrassing it would be to see him again in company with Toby. How was I going to hide my feelings? And would Guy start on about it again the minute he got me alone?

Well, I must just make sure that he never did get me alone, that was all.

By the time the taxi stopped outside Raymond Mansions I still felt stunned, and could not think of anything else, but I had at least made up my mind about three things.

(1) I would never tell Toby.

(2) I would never be alone with Guy.

(3) I did believe Guy loved me—or genuinely thought he did—and that it wasn't a frightful kind of joke.

I don't know why—something in his expression and one

or two of the things he had said, particularly *I've tried—I have, I swear it.*

Because Guy is usually absolutely never serious and this was the first time I had ever seen him so, and it had rung home.

Oh—I remembered this as I was making my way past Mr. Pegram's door, which the children had already disfigured by scratching *Pegram go home* on the paint—(it not occurring to them that this *was* his home)—there was also that hinting remark about Mr. St. Merryn, about Toby having known him before we met him at the party.

If there's anything I do hate now, more than cold weather, it is *mysteries.* So boring, unless of course they are in a thriller. All the same, I cast my thoughts back to the evening when we had met him.

When I call him an old man I suppose he would only seem old to someone of my age. He was only elderly, really, and unusually well-dressed, quite a dandy, and he looked sad.

I did remember, now, that we were never actually introduced to him. At least, I didn't hear Toby being, though Toby did introduce me, when I came up to where they were standing chatting. And as Toby didn't say anything about him afterwards I took it for granted Mr. St. M. was a mere party acquaintance.

And I also remember being a bit surprised when Toby said he was running down to see him in the country. But I was so annoyed at Toby saying he didn't like me—when he only saw me for five minutes—that I forgot about my surprise.

There you are, you see. The minute you get on to a slight mystery or secret there are all these details, so difficult to remember, and put in plain sentences. So that you simply long to be describing a hat.

But that will do about Mr. St. M. for now. I supposed in a depressed way as I walked up the stairs that there *was* a slight mystery about him. And now goodness knew there was a *secret* about Guy and *another* mystery about Toby's being all of a sudden so moody and odd—

So you may imagine how delighted I was to see Toby pop smiling out of the bedroom the instant I got into the flat, wearing one of his own dress shirts and his dress trousers and hear him shout in his gayest tone, "Step on it, Idle! We're going out."

"Who with?" I asked, beginning to sparkle in spite of everything. He looked so angelic.

"The Rodes, of course. Dinner. Then the premiére of *Space High*."

"Isn't that all about satellites and so forth?"

"Yes and absolutely everyone will be there."

This is almost Toby's favourite thing. And I must say I like it myself—poor, poor us.

But to get on.

We went, and it was dreamy, and I was able to put the one secret and the two slight mysteries to the back of my mind. I do not like all this about space, which bores me unless the moon is shining, but it certainly was dreamy.

Except for a moment half-way through the show when something, said on the stage perhaps, reminded me that there was yet another mystery or secret, that of old Mrs. Sweeting and those Roadknights.

Going home in The Car after the Rodes had driven off in their taxi, I suddenly decided to risk how he might take the story, and tell Toby.

You see, I felt bad because I could never tell him about Guy, and because I needed advice. I thought, I'll tell him, and at least there will be *one* secret the less.

"Toby," I began, "you know old Mrs. Sweeting."

"I remember her. I don't like the idea that I *know* her."

"Don't be a pomp, honey, because it doesn't suit you. Well, you remember me staying behind that day to comfort her?" I asked.

"Yes. I thought at the time you might have got something out of her. But there was so much else going on I forgot to ask you. Well?"

I might have *known* he would suspect something. And I felt quite shivery at the idea that he might suspect about Guy.

"I didn't get much, really. But she did tell me something." And I went on to tell him every word she had said.

To my surprise he laughed quite a lot. When I asked him what he was going to do, he said, "Oh, nothing, I think. We'll just go on hunting down ancestors, and if we come across this change of name, we'll take it in our stride. *I* can't help it. If people haven't portraits of their ancestors, or family houses, or papers going back four or five generations they must expect this kind of thing to turn up."

"Do you think they'd mind?"

"Shouldn't think so for a moment. Highwaymen are old enough to be romantic."

"She did say rick-burning and poaching."

"Those are only English rural peccadillos. Quite picturesque too, since the country became mechanized."

"Suppose a psychopathic murderer turned up?"

"Well, that wouldn't be so good. We might have to suppress him."

We drove on, and I felt more comfortable. Toby had not been cross with me for having a secret, nor had he suggested getting money for it from the Rodes. But I was also thinking that just as psychopathic murderers seem *really* frightening to us to-day, so must highwaymen have seemed really frightening and not romantic at all to our ancestors, and those Vikings, I suppose, to the characters who lived in Abbotstower.

"How do you think we're doing with them, so far?" Toby asked suddenly. "The Rodes."

"Very nicely, I should say. Gorgeous hot meals and lots of shows and twenty guineas a week."

"Oh yes. But I meant—taking the long view."

This is not a thing that comes naturally to a person at seventeen and a half. (Besides, my family never did. Even Aunt Edie used to say one might as well enjoy oneself as one is a long time dead—I say even, as she sometimes goes to Church. So I had no examples to follow.)

"I hadn't thought about that," I said, in confession, "How do you mean exactly, darling?"

"Well, do you see any hope of them taking us back to the States?"

"Is it warm there?"

"Nancy, I wish you would just *try* to—to be a little more intelligent. *Is it warm there!* Don't you know one single thing about the climate of America?"

"No," I said, in a defiant and sulky sort of voice, "Why should I?"

"Because—well, surely at school—and there are the newspapers—"

"I don't read the newspapers, except the fashion bits."

"I sometimes wonder what you do do," Toby muttered.

I could have said that I mended our clothes, as beautifully as a nun. But I didn't.

I also could have said that I wondered what he and Guy did, all those long hours they spent together. But I said absolutely nothing.

"But we're getting side-tracked," said Toby, more kindly,

93

"I've been thinking. I don't want us landed at the end of the summer with no money and no prospects."

"We never do have any," I said.

He glanced at me, smiling. But he said, in a kind of tone I couldn't analyse—

"Do you mind, honeypot?"

I shook my head.

"No longings for a little house somewhere in the new suburbs, with a garden?"

"No. Never." I shook my head. "So long as I've got you and it's a warm day and I can have a good hot meal I don't want anything."

I thought he was going to take his hands off the wheel and seize me. But instead he looked at me in that strange sorrowful way I'd seen before and said:

"You're a good little thing. I'm bloody lucky to have you. Only don't be too easily contented, lovey. That never gets you anywhere."

We were quiet for a little while. I did wonder what was the matter with my Toby. The painful thought then struck me that *perhaps he was beginning to get old*? After all, twenty-six is not exactly young. But of course I could never mention that. It is unavoidable, like an earthquake. Also tactless, as people do hate it.

"Oh well, something will turn up, I expect," he said at last.

But not quite as gaily as he used to when we were just married, and that crazy old Hon. Mrs. Beltringham took us for a gorgeous honeymoon to Madeira.

Afterwards, she never answered Toby's letters or 'phone calls.

"But I want us to start getting more intimate with the Rodes from now on," he was saying. "*You* might get her to talk about the boy occasionally, and show sympathy."

That would be their son, killed in that tiny war somewhere.

94

I told him that I would, though I hate talking about people who are dead, and to keep on sympathizing is most exhausting.

"And I'll find out what I can about his interests and income," Toby went on, "only it's damned difficult finding *anything* out about these Rodes, you know. They're rather mysterious. They have this place up in Maine, Sheldon Springs, near the Canadian border. I've seen snapshots of it. It's quite modest—(not by English standards, of course, it's fairly impressive by those)—spacious and pleasant but not palatial. And yet quite large sums of money seem to mean nothing to them."

"Perhaps they've been saving up for simply years and are now having a spending spree and will end up without a *dime*," I said—not helpfully, I will admit.

"I hope to God not. Our autumn plans will look pretty silly, in that case."

I said I expected it would be all right, which remark seemed to irritate Toby again. He got all right during the night. But I was beginning to worry about him.

Me, who had never worried in my life. More and more did I want someone to talk to.

X

THE last chapter being all mysteries and secrets and descriptions of peoples' worried feelings, I suppose can hardly be called a chapter at all, as nothing happens. So it will be a relief to tell you how I went to see Aunt Edie.

Not that it did any good.

In those old books my mother had, and Aunt Edie too, there was sometimes a wise ancient character or a clergyman or doctor who helped some young person with advice. Patting them. And either telling them to trust in God or put their shoulder to the wheel. But nowadays it is my experience that everyone is simply so busy they have not an instant to pat anyone, nor even to think about what is being said to them; being so occupied with thinking of what they must do next.

And as for telling God, I am certain that even to learn to tell takes quite some time, as this is getting to be a forgotten art, unless you are rather lucky.

Of course in my case there were all the oldies living round about us, unemployed, and with masses of leisure, and all quite kind. But Toby had rather cooled off Mr. Pegram for some reason—he does that, if he thinks people aren't going to come in useful and I shrank—(what a queer word— *shrank*, it sounds like a sea monster)—from telling Miss de Havilland because she was a Catholic and would take a religious point of view. Mrs. Rawlings would be sure to put me on to those Rays. And what help would they be, I ask you?

So there was only Aunt Edie.

Toby is resigned to me seeing her every two months or so, though he never will come too. He cannot stand her having a budgie whose name is Willy, I mean, he cannot stand her having a budgie *at all*, it wouldn't matter what its name was. So he has only seen her once, at our wedding, and I have always remembered that at the reception Guy was nice to her.

She has never quite got over Mrs. Raven managing everything for me when I was left an orphan, I think. She never says anything, but I am sure she minds.

So one morning I told Toby I was going to see her and he nodded and said all right, had I enough money, honey, and I said oh yes heaps thank you, blessing, and off I went. He was going motor-racing with Guy.

There was rather a maze of buses to be taken to get out to Aunt Edie's, which lies outside a village outside the town of Bedford, but I was lucky, and just before one o'clock I was walking down a quiet sunny lane between hedges, towards the hidden river. Out of the hedges all kinds of early summer flowers, mostly pale green or white, were drooping or springing, and already the air smelt of summer. There were also bees, and wasps, and all kinds of gauzy creatures very busy with their own concerns, and there were glimpses far off of silent green meadows under the burningly blue sky. The sun was positively flashing, high up there.

First there were some comfortable ordinary houses, all different, standing back from the widening lane at different lengths, and then I had to go down a narrower lane, shady and even a little damp, where meadowsweet grew. (I remember that name because on the cover of one of my mother's favourite old books there was a picture-flower of the title, *Meadowsweet*. I don't remember the writer's name, I never can.) Then I had to go along a little path of cobblestones, in front of four tiny cottages. Aunt Edie's was the last in the row.

Her front door was shut. But it always was because everyone used the back. This was round a teeny path at the side of the cottage, next to a stone wall over which you looked into a little green shady forest.

I expect you are thinking this sounds as if I do like the country. But if it had been a cold day my account of it all would be gloomy and quite different. Naturally even the country is all right if it is a warm day, because everywhere is.

Round the corner you came out into blazing sunlight again, and saw Auntie Edie's little kitchen garden, sloping down towards the river quite hidden in big silvery willow trees. The cobbled path began again and I went round it to her opened back door. I did like the openness, and the gently blazing sunlight, and the glow of green over fields and trees. For once, I would be sorry to go indoors.

I could hear Willy gobbling away to himself and Aunt Edie, talking to one of her possessions as she always does.

"You think because I've just paid fifteen and six to have you mended that you can do anything you choose, don't you? Well, you can just put that idea right out of your head. You're here to iron my clothes, not scorch them, and that's what you'll do. So we had better get that absolutely straight between us."

I walked round the door and said, "Hello Auntie."

"Nancy!" she said, looking up from the ironing board. "Well, here's a surprise. The last person I expected to see." She came across to me and we kissed. "Take your hat off, I wonder you can stand a hat, this lovely day, I never do, but of course I remember now *he* makes you. Aren't you hot?"

"Yes I am but I adore it." I sat down in a comfortable old chair full of dingy cushions. (Dingy I mean because of age. Faded is perhaps a better word.) "How are you, Auntie?"

I said somewhere farther back, Auntie Edie is an absolutely ordinary cheerful person of sixty-seven. My mother was the pretty one.

She has permanently waved grey hair in a short curly cut,

98

and a roundish, pinkish face with glasses, and dentures. She wears a flowered rayon dress in summer—when there is any —and a woollen jumper and skirt and a cardigan in winter.

I sometimes think that if I were to be in a crowd and she was there too I wouldn't recognize her. And yet I would, you know. There is something that makes her Auntie Edie and not just like a sheep or a hen or a Chinese. The nuns would say it was her "unique soul". But enough of religion, which you do not want to spoil a warm day with.

"Oh I'm all right. A bit of rheumatism in my knee but that comes of living on top of the river, and I wouldn't change. You look very nice. It's quite a blessing to see you in something light instead of that everlasting black. How are things going?"

"Oh, all right—quite well, really," and I explained about the Rodes, toning it down a little, of course, as it did sound rather uncertain and peculiar.

Now here I must explain that Auntie Edie has the wrong idea about Toby and me, believing firmly that I am dying to start a baby and settle down in a little house, with Toby in a regular job.

I am *not*, and I have told her so, as plainly as I can. But she persists in thinking that Toby is a selfish brute dragging me along in a life which I secretly hate.

When I had finished, Auntie Edie looked at me.

"And no sign of a family, I suppose?"

I shook my head, rather sulkily.

"Well, early days yet. But you're longing for one, I know." And she smiled and nodded *her* head, in a maddening sort of way.

"No I *am not*. Good heavens, I'm not eighteen yet." (Not that I would want one if I were forty-eight.)

"There's no good heavens about it. Why, in my work, I was *always* delivering girls of seventeen, eighteen, nineteen, with their first. Splendid little mothers some of them made, too. But now about lunch. There isn't much, I'm afraid. But I can always open a tin, not that I like them."

This usual muddle about the baby had not been a good beginning, I felt. Because if Auntie Edie was so mistaken about that, what wise advice could she give about the secrets and mysteries?

There wasn't much for lunch. But Auntie E. is a good cook and she made the best of what there was, and we picked vegetables fresh from the garden, and I forgot the irritating opening to the visit.

But after lunch when we were sitting with our cups of tea in the sun, I found it not easy to start telling her. She was still slightly fussed because I had insisted on our sitting on the back doorstep, "like gipsies", she said. But it would have been sinful to waste that heavenly warmth inside the small and heavily furnished cottage.

However, here we went.

"Auntie," I began, "I've really come to ask your advice."

She looked at me kindly over the top of her cup but said nothing, and I went on carefully, having decided that the thing to do was to tell her only about Guy. There, she might give some help. But if I told her about all the other little irritating puzzles, what help could she give? You really needed someone whom I saw almost every day, with whom I could report and discuss.

I got it all out about Guy, with many cries of "No!", and "There's impudence for you" and so forth from her, and I ended up with, "And what I am really wondering is, shall I tell Toby?"

"Yes, of course. I should think so, indeed. The minute you get home," said Auntie Edie, firmly and without taking an instant to ponder over the matter. I was sure that she had made up her mind while I was still speaking.

"But, Auntie, it would hurt his feelings dreadfully. He's so fond of Guy, he's his oldest friend and his best one."

"He'll soon get over *that*, when he hears what a creature he is. Besides, your husband. You shouldn't have any secrets from your husband. It's his duty to protect you."

"I can protect myself. At least, usually I feel I can. But sometimes I get rather scarey. Suppose I don't tell Toby, and by some awful chance he were to *find out*?"

"Well that's just it."

"He might believe I'd been having an affair with Guy, and that's why I'd kept the whole thing dark."

"Isn't that what I'm saying?"

"All the same—" I said, and drank some tea and looked away across the green meadows, sleepy and still in the afternoon light.

I couldn't see it all as plainly as Auntie thought she saw it. I knew how fond Toby was of Guy.

"That nice young fellow. Such a gentleman. I can't get over it. And you a mere child, and married. Well, I've always heard that the best of men are weak about sex," she was saying. "They are like that, and you have to face it."

"I can't tell him," I said suddenly, "and I won't.'"

"Then why ask my advice, if you've made up your mind not to take it?" Auntie Edie said, not crossly, because she is really fond of me, I think, but in a calmly sensible voice.

"Oh, well. You know. I just felt I must talk to someone."

"Your husband is the right one to talk to."

"I suppose he is. But—" and then rather before I knew it, I was telling her about Toby having seemed less gay, and slightly worried, lately.

But as soon as I had, I was sorry. Because she at once nodded, in a triumphant way.

"I'm not at all surprised to hear that, Nancy. He *is* beginning to worry. And why? Because his conscience is commencing to prick him, and he feels he ought to give you a nice home, and let you have that dear little baby."

I really almost gritted my teeth, except that I had never done it before and it would feel peculiar. But I said nothing. Auntie Edie wanted me to want a baby (why do people call them little, by the way? They always are, and surely it could be taken for granted by now?) and simply nothing, not an earthquake or a revolution or a war or *anything*, would make her believe I didn't.

"I don't think it's that," I said at last.

"Well I'm sure it is," Auntie said in a flat *that's that* sort of voice, stubbing out her cigarette, and got up from the step. "Now I'm just going to do this bit of washing-up, and then I'm going to take you in next-door-but-one, to see Linda Smith's baby."

I had been faintly aware of distant baby noises from time to time—but hadn't of course given them one thought.

"I'll help you," I said, beginning to get up.

"No, dear, I can manage. It's a lovely day and I don't expect you get much rest, stuck up there in London. You have a little holiday."

So I sat in the sunlight, smoking, and simply putting all worries, mysteries and problems out of my mind. I could hear Auntie Edie in the background, talking now and then to the washing-up.

"That's a nice thing to have on you, I must say, egg. I washed you thoroughly enough this morning. *Come* off, will you? Obstinate. That's right, now fall into the water again and crack something, I would, if I were you, so helpful."

It was a kind of mutter, rather soothing really, to listen to while you sat sleepily in the hot sun, and though I know some people would think Auntie was mental, she was not in the least, being as I have said the most ordinary person I know, and this talking to unliving objects was her only peculiar point.

It came of living alone. I suppose if you are old and live alone you get like that, strange in some way. You see, Mrs. Rawlings had these Rays, and Mr. Pegram had his dog on a record-player, and Miss de Havilland would have had something if she hadn't been a Catholic. And I suppose some people would say believing in saints and God and Our Lady was a kind of strange habit.

I am so thankful I have Toby.

My thoughts went off into a kind of warm dream, and after a bit Auntie Edie came out, taking off a plastic apron.

"We'll just go round to Linda's now. Rock will have had his sleep, bless him."

"After Rock Hudson," I said, getting up.

"Yes. Poor Linda, she used to be so fond of her pictures. But of course she's given all that up long ago."

So likely, this remark, to make a person want a baby of their own. Not that I have an absolute passion for the cinema.

"Can't they ever get a baby sitter?" I asked, being polite, as we made our way along the warm cobblestones.

"Oh Linda'd never trust anybody else with Rock. I do have him for an hour in the afternoon sometimes while she goes into Bedford to see the shops. But he's never really taken to me, he's Linda's boy."

She can have him, I thought, and very welcome. I suppose she thought a sitter would murder him, and after seeing him I would hardly blame one.

He looked rather like a rock, a great, fat, scornful rock, red with being asleep, and all over crumbs. Though he was nicely kept, and so was Linda, poor soul, in a clean sun-dress and her hair set in almost the latest fashion, and her cottage was very pretty, brightly papered, a different one on each wall, with indoor plants and blue and pink rubberoid tiles on the floor and simply spotless, and full of sun.

It was like a doll's house, except for awful Rock, who glared at us out of blue eyes all creased up in fat and then turned away his huge bald head and howled.

"He doesn't like visitors," said Linda, picking him up and cuddling him, "naughty boy, aren't you?"

It was an unfortunate baby to choose, if Auntie Edie wanted me to envy Linda, because I thought he was the absolute and final end, though Auntie Edie and Linda kept telling him he was gorgeous. It had no effect, of course, though something did stop him roaring, and I kept thinking, if he is what they call gorgeous, *what would a baby they thought rather awful be like?*

But I supposed they never did think a baby was awful.

I could see Linda staring at me and my nails and hair, and I knew she didn't like me much. But she was polite and kind, giving us more tea and some of a cake she had made herself, from a recipe in a woman's paper.

It was all boring and pleasant, and it passed the time until I said that I was afraid I must go now.

Fortunately Auntie Edie is not one of those elderly people who beg and implore you not to go yet on their bended knees. She got up briskly at once and said yes, there was a bus from the corner in twenty minutes and she would walk up with me, and then there was a slight scene when Linda said, Rock kiss Auntie Nancy bye-bye, and Auntie Nancy smiled bravely but her very soul fainted within her, as I once read in one of Mum's old books, and she thanked heaven when Rock took one look at her sweet gypsy face and bellowed.

What with being kissed by people of a hundred, and being asked to kiss horrible babies, I felt that I was decidedly off kissing anyone but my Toby, and how I longed to get back to him!

I was half expecting Auntie to tell me to kiss Willy bye-bye, but she isn't like that, as I ought to have remembered. She said in a commonplace voice, "Willy, say bye-bye to Nancy," and Willy churned about in his seed bin and gobbled —with which performance Auntie Edie seemed satisfied. She said that often he was as clear as clear, and once when she was sitting shelling peas he flew on to her shoulder and said, "What are you doing?"

This was a bit too much. I know Aunti Edie is truthful as the day but she must have dreamed it.

"Well, thank you for your advice, Auntie," I said as we walked up the hot sweet-smelling lane to the bus stop. It wasn't wise to dig up the subject again, perhaps, but I had an unsatisfied feeling.

I had screwed myself up to come here and ask her, and it had all been over almost at once. I am not a person who enjoys chewing, but she might have shown a bit more interest.

I felt utterly un-advised.

"That's all right, Nancy. But if you value advice, you should take it. I'm sure I'm right."

You or anyone else can be *sure* they are, I thought, without *being*.

"You see, it's all—" I was beginning when she interrupted. "Yes, dear, well I'm sure it'll all come right when that baby comes along. Now here's the bus. Don't forget—book to The Plasterers, and then turn left and cross the road and get the Diggenham bus outside Carters."

She gave me a quick kiss and I hopped on to the bouncing green country bus and off we went.

I looked back to wave, and Auntie Edie, would you imagine, was already walking quickly away. When she had not seen me, her only niece or nephew, for two months. She might at least have given a wave. I wondered for a minute if she was permanently offended about Mrs. Raven, but then I thought, it's just Auntie Edie, who is one of those few elderly people who *do* have plenty to think about—those Meals-on-Wheels, and her church, and knitting for a firm that sells hand-made things, and selling goods for a mail-order firm, and her friends, and so forth. I suppose you should be thankful for such an elderly relation, not lonely, or hanging on you. But I still did think she might out of mere politeness have waved.

And do you know, after all my being annoyed because of her saying Toby was worrying about our life, she was right.

Wasn't it maddening?

XI

OF course, I came home more decided not to tell Toby than ever. Auntie Edie's advice seemed to have made my own feeling against telling him all the stronger.

Well, after this, we had a nice time for nearly three weeks.

No cloud darkened the horizon (I like to put in something like that now and then. It is called a metaphor—I think). The weather was lovely, warm and soft by day and by night, and we saw a lot of the Rodes. Toby came back rather glum from seeing that elderly Mr. St. Merryn, and said he might not be seeing him again because he was touchy, and would not come in useful.

I thought, oh well, good, St. Merryn is out, and forgot him.

And after a few days, during which Toby warned me that there would now be no more Reserve Fund because his bit of capital was exhausted, he cheered up.

After all, we had twenty guineas a week. Out of this, Guy had to have five for The Car, and Toby had to pay for tickets into castles and so forth, but it was an understood gentleman's agreement that the Rodes paid for all lunches and teas and drinks—except sometimes for politeness's sake—and of course they took us out to dreamy evening entertainments. In the front stalls usually. And to the Flower Show, where Mrs. Rode nearly went crazy because she practically worshipped flowers, like some people do dogs or cats. I had to buy another hat—unheard of—because we were so socially busy, to have two at a time to make a change.

We saw Guy sometimes. Once or twice he had lunch with us and the Rodes, and I felt embarrassed but he was cool and unashamed—and even looked at me a lot, in the old way. Sometimes I wondered that Toby did not notice. But of course if a thing is almost impossible, it doesn't enter your head, and you don't notice.

Guy's mysterious friend who owned our flat had disappeared in Algeria, so Guy said, and until he came back or wrote, his affairs were held up and no-one claimed the place. So that was goody again.

It was July, now, and we saw a lot of the English countryside. We did not always go ancestor-hunting but sometimes to places afar off. The Rodes liked going to popular beautiful places where everybody goes, and Toby often groaned to me about this in secret. So we went to many gorgeous ancient houses in the deep country, one was called Blenheim and one was called Owlpen, I remember, and also Hatfield quite near London where you can see a pair of stockings that belonged to the other Queen Elizabeth, and also her garden hat.

I cannot help writing something about these stockings because they interested me more than the pictures or the architecture or anything.

They were knitted in yellowy silk, quite coarsely knitted. But I expect they seemed wonderfully fine to Queen E. because in those days all the stockings were wool, and I was wondering tremendously, while looking at them, *what* she would have thought of twelve-denier nylons? I shall always remember those yellowy ancient stockings.

Her garden hat looked fairly modern.

We also went, imagine, to The Tower of London and Toby hated this almost enough to tell the Rodes he did, saying to me afterwards that to go there was the ultimate and final end, only National School children parties went, and people so peculiar as to be practically loony. Mr. Rode prowled for hours in the Weapons room, looking at old American pistols used against the Redskins. We thought he would never weary of them.

But we also went to every castle in Sussex. I never saw so many grand ancient trees in my life, and to stay for three days so that we could see Kenilworth, and also on a tour to see a lot of rugged old castles in Wales. Toby never cares, poor love, to be far from London and he was afraid that the Rodes would drag us away to Ireland to see some bog, where a fairy shoe was said to have been found. This utter superstitious nonsense, however, did not trigger them off, and if we had gone it would have been Toby's own fault, as he dug up the story in some magazine and told them about it thinking they would enjoy a bit of Irish quaintery.

But they only said things about prehistoric psychology.

As well as having such a nice time, I was beginning to think Guy might have got over his feelings. Or perhaps he never had them at all but said so to annoy me. Or perhaps it was one of his jokes. Anyway, after my first anxiety, I now began to forget that afternoon at the Tate Picture Gallery, and my worries gradually dwindled off in the warm weather.

But one thing I had quite forgotten.

I had not been alone with Guy since that afternoon. And one evening—

But I will tell you how it came about.

XII

I HAD to give several hours once a week to beautifying myself
—nails, sometimes hair, skin, eyebrows, mending, brushing,
and so forth. But in this particular week we had been out so
much in the day that only evenings were left, and as Toby
was going out with Guy, and we had no engagement with
the Rodes, one Thursday I decided to get my beautifying
done.

By eight o'clock hair, nails and toes were finished. I was
sitting looking at *Vogue*, and drinking black coffee, with my
face covered in a green-white mask of beauty clay, when the
'phone rang.

I was annoyed, because my hands would leave clayey
marks on the thing. Also, as of course everybody knows,
when your face is done with that stuff it cracks off if you
talk or smile. (When I say "everybody" I mean most people,
not the Prime Minister, or vicars.) Also I wanted to look at
Vogue.

"Darling Nancy," said Guy's pleased voice which I heard
with surprise, thinking that he was safe with Toby. "Is Toby
there?"

"No," I said, before I could think not to. "Er—no, he isn't."

"You're alone, then?"

I should have said, No, I'm having an oldie in for coffee,
any minute. But instead I said,

"Yes—isn't he with you?"

"No. Oh, all right, I'll try Randy's place—I'm sorry to have
bothered you, darling Nancy," and he rang off.

Randy was Randolph Brooks, another of their mysterious

buddies. He was something to do with advertising, and he had a horrid little flat, all damp and full of bits of old family furniture in a thin dark house off St. James's Street, W., and his family despaired of him. I went back to my coffee and *Vogue*.

Would you imagine a person could be so non-sophisticated? Because in twenty minutes or so when the front door bell rang, I swore, this time, thinking it was an oldie coming to borrow tea, or flour for one of the endless cakes they were always making (scorning shop ones, as they all did), but then I thought, oh well, poor old thing, and went to the door.

And of course it was Guy.

He started when he saw me, and then he smiled. He had put on a pitiful look, as I opened the door, but this now vanished.

"Darling Nancy, how sweet you look," and though I cannot say that he actually pushed past me, before I knew it he was in the hall. I was so fussed that I could only lead the way to the living-room, inwardly calling upon the ancestresses.

"I must apologise," I said hardly able to move my lips and therefore speaking in a very peculiar voice. "I wasn't expecting visitors, and this is my beauty-cult evening."

"Oh do you have a beauty-cult?" He sat down and leant back, looking at me hard. "I say," beginning to laugh, "I'm awfully sorry, but you do look so hideous! No one would believe you're unusually dishy."

I stood there, covered in green clay, with a stiff face. I felt —helpless is the only word. It was a most unpleasant feeling. I was getting a little frightened, too. He was now staring hard.

"This is to do my skin good," I said, sitting down. "I can't move my mouth properly."

"I know, darling Nancy. I knew a girl once—can you imagine?—who used to use that stuff."

I stared into the silent gas fire, whose coppery face stared back at me. Make conversation, say *anything*, advised the ancestresses. But it was so difficult to move my mouth. And this seemed to make it difficult to think of anything to say. He was silent now, just looking at me. The quiet in the room grew deeper.

"I'll just wash this off—the ten minutes is up," I said suddenly, and hurried into the kitchen. While I was scrubbing my face with a tea towel—so bad for it and I was furious—I listened with every ear. But not a sound.

It takes ages to get that stuff off. Why I didn't go into the *bathroom* was because it was buried in the heart of the flat, the farthest room from the front door, and I had a feeling that no one could get at me quickly to rescue me, if Guy came after me.

But he was still sitting, looking pitiful, now.

"That's better," I said out of my glowing face "I'm sorry about these," and I moved my head which was all over pink and blue rollers.

He didn't say anything. Only looked. Really it was depressing. I tried again.

"Did you want Toby about anything important?"

"I don't want Toby at all." It came out a kind of growl. Then he seemed to wake up. "Actually they're rather becoming," he said, "like a halo or something." He looked round the room, in a desolate way.

"Would you like some coffee?" I said.

He shook his head. Staring again, now.

"Then I'm afraid I must—I mean, I'm going to bed," I said firmly—to my own utter horror, as I heard these absolutely fatal words pass my lips—*now you've done it, Nancy Régine*, shouted all the ancestresses in chorus. Oh, you *mutton-head. Espèce d'imbécile!*

Guy got up from the chair.

"Darling Nancy," he said, "there is nothing I should like better."

I didn't move. He stood there, looking at me.

"If you touch me, I shall bite you," I said. "As hard as I can." (Screams can be muffled but seldom teeth.)

He shrugged. "That wouldn't stop me. I shouldn't notice," he said. "But I'm not going to try violence. We'll play fair." (He was walking a little nearer to me while he was speaking, and I was beginning to feel strangely like a rabbit under a snake or something.) "I'll start by telling you a few things about old Toby that I think you should know. You're his wife, as you don't hesitate to remind me. When you've heard them, you may feel differently about him."

"I know everything about Toby," I said.

Guy's eyes were now shining on me like two glasses of sherry.

I am sorry if this sounds peculiar. I set out to write the truth, and that was just what they made me think of—two glasses of sherry, held up against the light, on some desperate occasion with people drinking a last toast before a hopeless rally or so forth. Because they did look fierce and reckless.

Before I knew it, he had grabbed me. I just had time to gasp—"You said you wouldn't," when he shut me up with a horrid moustachy toothy kiss.

I jerked my head away, seized his hand, and bit it just as hard as I could bite. "Take that," I said, as he snatched it away and stood staring. "Thought you said you wouldn't notice," I went on, in a kind of panting jeer.

The ancestresses were forgotten. It was funny, I felt as if I were back at school again, suddenly much younger, and spiteful.

"You meant it," he said at last, in a dazed voice, and just then there was a knock at the front door.

I jumped, but felt a rush of relief. Guy was wrapping up

his hand in his handkerchief. Across the skin on the back were two white bruised-looking half-circles.

" 'Tisn't old Toby, he'd have a key," he said, following me as I leapt towards the door. No, no such luck as its being *old Toby*. And would I refrain from telling him about this? Oh would I *not*!

Hardly knowing what I was doing, I was so furious, I flung open the door. And there was Mrs. Rawlings.

She was dressed in a man's ancient dressing-gown of faded grey and yellow plaid, and her head was tied up in an old bit of Indian stuff, all over scraps of looking-glass, and she was holding out a little blue bowl with "Rhoda" on it white letters.

"There you are, dear child," she began, smilingly. "I must apologise—I came to borrow a mouthful of Rice Krispies. But what dreadful vibrations!" And the smile faded.

"Oh do come in! Yes, of course. I'll just get them, but won't you stay and have some coffee? I was just going to make some, that is, we——" I babbled, almost seizing the old thing in my relief. "*Do* come in. And *do* excuse my appearance." I smiled like a searchlight.

She shook her head, staring up into the air above me.

"You are very kind, dear child, but what *have* you been doing? Not skinning a rabbit, I hope? Or boiling a live lobster? The vibrations are simply stifling. I can scarcely breathe. And *shocking* colours."

"I'm awfully sorry—I'll open a window," I stammered. In my relief at seeing her, I had forgotten her peculiar beliefs. "But *do* come in."

"Oh, I couldn't enter a flat where there are vibrations of that kind, dear child. It would upset me for days. I am only glad that you cannot see them, dark brown, and red, a dreadful angry red, and quantities of the most *appalling* purple. (I should be sorry indeed to tell you what *They* mean.) What have you been doing? Not sitting alone with your thoughts surely?"

"No, oh no—a—a friend of my husband's came in unexpectedly, and we were—arguing. About politics," I ended, distractedly, but thinking this last lie was rather a masterstroke. (The ancestresses, no doubt.)

"Oh fatal, dear child. Nothing produces such bad vibrations as impassioned argument."

I could *feel* Guy, lurking in the inner room, and no doubt sucking his hand.

"I must try to contact the Rays," Mrs. Rawlings was saying, and plainly getting ready to push off.

"Oh, but—what—do just let me get the Krispies, won't you?" I almost gasped, and determined not to let her go unless Guy went too.

"I am sorry, but I could not eat a cereal that has been exposed to those vibrations." She shook her bits of looking-glass.

"They've been in the refrigerator," I said, suddenly remembering this strange fact. It was true, too; I'd spilt a lot and scooped them up into a bowl and put them in there. "Would that help?"

"Ah. It might. The vibrations, unfortunately, can get in anywhere. Bars and bolts mean nothing to them. But of course the element of *protection*, existing, in however debased a form, in the minds of those who designed the refrigerator, could exert a beneficial effect. Evil vibrations would retreat!" She waved her fingers, in a dramatic kind of way. "Baffled! I really think that we might venture, dear child."

So far, so good, as they say. But first I was going to get rid of Guy.

There had been silence from the living-room.

Now I went a little way along the passage and called in a firm kind of voice:

"Guy. Come and meet Mrs. Rawlings."

There was no answer. Sulking. Mrs. R. was still hovering on the doorstep, staring, and moving her head round as if she were following the movements of something up in the air. It really was creepy, and what with this, and Guy, how I longed for Toby to come home you cannot *imagine*.

"You'll like Guy," I hurried on, "he's a very famous racing motorist— —"

"I am always glad to widen my knowledge of this world's inhabitants, dear child, and I have never met a racing-motorist, but— —"

Guy was coming slowly across the hall. I turned to him.

"Oh . . . here is Mr. Murray. Guy, this is my neighbour and good friend, Mrs. Rawlings . . . we were just wondering if the Rice Krispies are all right . . ." I said somewhat wildly. (He really did look *murderous*, that was the word that came into my head.) "Mrs. Rawlings says our little argument has filled the flat with the most frightful vibrations," I went on.

"Blackish-purple. Quite frightening," put in Mrs. R.

"Oh? Are you keen on the Occult?" said Guy, managing to put on a social voice, "so is my grand-mother. But I'm afraid it's all a bit above my head."

This fitted in so well with Mrs. R.'s gazings up at the ceiling that I had to choke back a hysterical kind of laugh.

Guy hadn't looked at me, and he was keeping his hand down at his side.

"I am more than 'keen'. It is my strongest interest . . . what have you done to your hand, Mr. Murray?"

As she couldn't see it, I supposed that those Rays must have drawn her attention to it. But if there were purple vibrations buzzing round it, like mosquitoes, I think it was tactless of the Rays.

"Oh—it's nothing, thanks, a friend's . . . dog . . . bit it."

I think he meant another word than *dog* and I was inwardly furious.

"Would you like me to relieve the pain? It looks exceedingly painful."

How she knew this I didn't know, as she couldn't see it.

"Awfully kind of you but please don't trouble."

"It would be no trouble. I like to 'keep my hand in' as they say of cake-making. I could concentrate benevolent Rays upon it. I have known quite wonderful results with a sprained ankle."

"Oh please don't bother—I'm an earthy type, I'm afraid, and they might not work on me. Perhaps," glancing towards me, "if you have a little disinfectant——"

"I used the last drop this morning," I said. Not kindly, but really——!

Mrs. Rawlings was looking distressed. I suppose, what with Guy furious, and me furious, and both of us saying things *at* each other, the vibrations were getting worse.

"Well, I must go," Guy said. He turned to me "Good night, Nancy. Good night," smiling falsely at Mrs. R.

"Won't you wait and see Toby?" I said in an I-dare-you kind of voice, "he ought to be in any minute."

But he didn't answer. He smiled again—you would not have known he was angry, unless you knew his face as well as I did—and hurried down the stairs.

I suddenly felt awful. Tired and shaken up, and in a muddle.

"What?" I said to Mrs. R., who had said something.

"Poor boy."

"Poor boy!" I burst out. "If you *knew*——"

She stood there in her dressing-gown and her head-scarf all over looking-glass, looking at me mildly. It was all so dotty

and awful that I could have *screamed*. Oh, where was Toby?
How I hate serious things, only I and Toby know.

I sat despairingly down on the stairs.

"Yes," nodded Mrs. Rawlings, "what is needed now is a cup
of tea."

She began to lead the way downstairs, and, having slammed
my front door and shut myself out, as I suddenly realised, I
had to follow her. I remembered that this was the first time,
since I had known him, that Guy had said just "Nancy"
without the "darling". I don't know why this made me feel
worse.

And, imagine, it wasn't true tea at all but some ghastly
herbal brew, dark green, out of a packet with the Signs of the
Zodiac on it—I remembered Mrs. Raven telling my fortune,
oh dear, happy days when I first knew Toby and there were
no mysteries or secrets or Guy—and it tasted of simply
nothing.

I sat in a broken old chair, off which Mrs. Rawlings had
pushed a pile of ancient books, and drank the stuff, which
thank heaven was at least scalding hot, and Mrs R. sat on an
old sofa covered with more books and sipped away, looking
into the blue flame of the oil heater, and we didn't talk.

And the extraordinary thing was that presently I did begin
to feel better. I don't mind my surroundings much, you know,
so long as it's warm. I dare say a lot of housewives would have
been horrified at Mrs. Rawlings's living-room, which was
lined on three sides with books up to the ceiling and so dusty
that everything was dulled with it. But it was cosy, somehow.
The light was soft, and there was a wonderful pink and yellow
rose, as big as a small cabbage, in a plain drinking glass standing on the table among masses of Pools forms and horse-
racing newspapers.

"What a gorgeous rose," I said at last.

She roused herself out of what I suppose was a *meditation*.

"Yes. That is 'Peace'. I often think, if the image is so beautiful, what must the prototype be?"

But I had had enough of that sort of thing for one evening, and I hadn't a clue what she meant and so I only gave a vague kind of smile.

I was trying to decide about something. I felt, now, that I *absolutely, simply, must talk to someone*. Aunt Edie had been no more good than a bilious attack, and so what about Mrs. Rawlings?

But then I though, no. She would only come up with Rays, and images, and vibrations, and Zodiac tea, and so forth.

As for telling Toby about this last incident, I did think of it, in my first anger, but now I saw that it could only make things worse.

Also—and this may sound funny to you—I felt in a way ashamed. It wasn't my fault, yet I did.

It was getting late and I was sleepy. So I got up, and said good night to Mrs. R., and thank-you for the horrid tea, and then, just as I was getting away, she stopped me in my tracks. She said:

"I'm concerned for Mr. Murray."

"Oh—I shouldn't bother, really," I muttered, tired out by now.

"He is in a bad way. Those dreadful vibrations—he was the source of them—or rather, they were attracted to him—and he was completely surrounded by them."

I didn't know what to say. I stood and stared at her.

"He does need help, you know," she went on, looking at me like an owl or something over the top of her glasses.

"I think he's quite able to help himself," I said. It was poor fussed me, and deceived "old Toby", who deserved sympathy, I thought.

She shook her head.

"No, dear child. You see, he is capable of evil. Some people are not, and they are all right, no matter what may happen to them through evil done by others. But your friend——"

"He isn't my friend, Mrs. Rawlings, he's a friend of my husband's."

"Well, he needs help. He needs it badly," she said, turning away. "I will see what can be done. Good night, dear child."

I went away, feeling flat out, and sat down on the stairs to doze until Toby came home. I needed help, too. And where was I going to get it?

XIII

PERHAPS you will not be surprised to hear that after this flare-up I did exactly nothing.

I didn't tell Toby. I didn't confide in anyone else. I just went on as usual, trying to put the whole business out of my mind.

I think the Rodes must have become slightly bored about this time, with driving to one spoilt village after another, pulling up at the same forlorn church standing back from the narrow High Street where the traffic panted and screeched (another word like a sea monster—or more like some tropical bird this time, perhaps), with the same smell of frying chips, and feeling of bustle and hurry.

We had hunted in ancient registers, and questioned old people living in tiny cottages in shabby back streets whether they remembered anyone named Rode until Toby and I, at least, were utterly weary of it. And we had had no more luck like that time at Waltham Cross.

I used to have a strange feeling, while we were standing outside some one-storey little place whose door opened straight on to the road, as if there was a huge mass of quietness and dullness, lying underneath all the bright shops and the noise and loud voices in the High Street, and that this was real, and the other was only a kind of varnish.

It was a disturbing feeling. I didn't like it. I suppose it was really a secret fear of getting old or dying or something. It was dim, and not strong, but—oh, I don't know. I can't write about it. I only know I used to be glad when we had left the dreary little cottages behind, what with shouting into deaf ears and trying not to stare rudely into poor little rooms, and worrying at confused old minds. I felt so sorry for some of those old people. They were being neglected.

I think the Rodes felt sorry for them, too, because Mr. Rodes always used to say after one of these interviews, that it amazed him that a nation like England, having the most advanced social services in the world except Sweden, should do so little for old people.

Toby used to drop remarks about "getting on with our good work" from time to time.

This wasn't because he felt the need to earn our twenty guineas "honestly". He has always made it clear to me that he never thinks about honesty, because times have changed, and honesty is out. (It was only an idea, anyway, he says). But he was afraid that if the Rodes' interest in the hunting wasn't kept alive, they would suddenly drop the whole thing, and then where would we be?

And the very next morning after this scene with Guy, when I woke up feeling still fussed, and Toby had one of his queer gloomy moods, they rang up to say, could we drive them out to a place called Harefield—in Herts, as usual. They'd met someone at a party whose retired solicitor lived there, and this retired solicitor was ninety and had lived in this house all his life and his father and grandfather too, and these people the Rodes met at the party had said Mr. Cranford was "a mine of local tradition".

"What an uncomfortable thing to be," I said, feeling that a laugh would not come amiss, ". . . a mine." Toby only swigged coffee and looked despondent.

"I feel this is breaking up," he said.

Never tell people to cheer up. It makes them worse. I fluffed out my hair, absent-mindedly, while I gazed at the dishy girls in *The Daily Mirror*—(which I *will have*, because I like it. Toby never reads a paper, relying for his information on knowledgeable characters met in smart bars, and so forth.

So his view of any crisis is different from the papers, being kind of *inside* and more exciting).

My hair had gone well, in spite of the scene with Guy. I had taken the rollers off, before I went to bed.

(Actually Toby thinks I look sweet in the rollers, and though I know the women's papers are always warning you never to let your husband see that kind of thing it seems to me that if a husband is going to pass out at the sight of a wife in rollers, he cannot be relied upon—which is what you need in a husband.)

No—I took the rollers off because they were v. uncomfortable to sleep in.

Toby gloomed on, and I looked at *The Daily Mirror* and wished that he would let me wear clothes like the girls in it do, and the dull heavy summer morning outside seemed to be standing still. At last I said—

"If you think they're losing interest, why not tell them about Roadknight? You know—the highwayman."

Toby shrugged and didn't answer. He really did look in the depths of depression.

"Toby," I said, deciding suddenly. "What's the matter?"

"Nothing. Forget it, Nancy."

"I'm sure something is. You're so peculiar lately."

He looked at me, in what I can only write of as a desperate way, but didn't say anything for a minute. Then he said slowly.

"It's nothing to get in a tizz about, darling. Just a number of small things that have been mounting up. They're on my nerves a bit."

"Can't you tell me about them?"

"There's nothing to tell, Idle. They're all small things. A different type wouldn't let them worry him."

"I do wish you'd tell me. My father used to say that I had

a good head on my shoulders, when I was very little. I might be able to *advise* you."

"There's nothing to *advise* about," he said, making a kissing face at me. "Nothing serious"—beginning to get up from the table—"Only some people don't realise that there are things a Public School man doesn't do. And I wish they would remember it. That's all."

"Don't fly off," I said, giving it up for the time being, "you haven't decided about Roadknight."

He sat down again, "No, I don't think we'll tell them. If we were going to, we ought to have done it at once, when the old woman told you. It would look peculiar—and it is peculiar, keeping it to ourselves all this time and bringing it out weeks afterwards. You ought to have told me at once, really, Nancy. Why didn't you?"

Now I really was in a difficult spot. Why hadn't I?

Because, among other slight fears, I had had the thought that my Toby might *use* this bit of ancient scandal. Try blackmailing the Rodes in fact.

I didn't answer.

"Why, Nancy?" he repeated.

He was on to it now, I could see. I lost my head, never having had any experience of managing a mass of secrets and mysteries, and said quickly——

"I was afraid you'd ask them for money."

The next instant I flung my arms round him. I couldn't bear the hurt expression of his mouth.

"Oh darling, darling, I didn't mean it. Truly I didn't."

But he put me away from him—Toby! I couldn't believe it was happening.

"So *you* think that's what I'm like, too, as well as everybody else?"

"I don't, I don't, truly. Oh please believe me. I did just think it for a moment, but only for a moment. I don't know why——"

He put his arms round me again. The hurt look had gone, and he had put on a serious and rather noble one. You know, I felt he had *put* it on, but the other look had been natural.

"You don't know much about men, you're so young, but haven't I told you again and again that there are things a Public School man doesn't do?"

"Yes. Oh yes, you have, often. I'm so sorry, darling Toby, darling——" and we passionately hugged.

So that was all right.

Or nearly all right. I didn't feel quite comfortable. I knew I'd hurt him, and I felt this would add to his secret worries. If he couldn't rely utterly on me, who could he rely on?

Oh, why do people have to hurt each other?

But of course we cheered up. I made some more coffee, which there was just time to drink before we left to fetch the Rodes, and on the way down into London we talked about them, and Roadknight, and our future.

Toby said that he had not succeeded in finding out anything about how much money the Rodes had. He would have had to put a private eye on them, he said, to find out anything that might come in useful and he just hadn't got the money. (Private eyes are expensive.) I felt that he hadn't *bothered* much about finding out, either, and I thought, that's because of his secret worry.

Because now I was certain that he had one.

And *I* confessed that I hadn't tried to keep Mrs. Rode sweet, with sympathy about her dead son and being *daughterly*. Somehow, I was always forgetting to. If she'd been an old b., it would have been easier, I think, but she was just an ordinary nice American woman, and when we were alone, which was hardly ever, we gossipped about clothes and differences in the English and American Way of Life, and I quite forgot.

So we both admitted that we were no further on in our chance of the Rodes practically adopting us. Come the end of the summer, and we should be at liberty again.

"At liberty" is a pretty way of saying we should have no regular money coming in and no prospects.

I didn't care. It was only July now, and anything could turn up. But I knew that Toby did mind.

As for Roadknight, we decided to do nothing about him. If we came across him in our search, well and good. Otherwise—nothing.

Boring, boring "homely, happy Herts". Same big trees, same main roads choked with traffic and little lanes ending in another main road, same crowded small towns and glammed-up villages. And in the poorer back streets old people in cramped cottages or bed-sitters, with people waiting for them to die so they could pounce on their former homes and glam them up too, and sell them for thousands.

I was probably depressed about Toby.

But this morning was not going to be the usual familiar programme.

Mr. Rode asked Toby to stop the car in a little place called Benfield, between Hertford and Ware. Toby obeyed, with an enquiring glance.

"We'll find a garage and park," Mr. Rode said. "The old man lives in the middle of the fields, way up on that ridge." He glanced up at some low hills, quite close at hand.

"Do you mean to say there isn't a road?" Toby asked, and I knew that he was trying not to sound sick, "how does he manage, at his age?"

"He walks, so I understand. There is a track to the house, on the other side of the ridge, but it's narrow and rough. I doubted whether The Car would enjoy it."

Toby got busy with finding a garage.

I wasn't looking forward to a walk, myself, because it was a cool blowy morning and my shoes were for town. So were Mrs. Rode's. But fortunately neither of us were wearing spike heels.

So off we went. Down a main road. Across it. Down a narrower but still noisy and crowded one. Petrol fumes puffed in our faces. Huge lorries banged and clattered at us. I can understand, you know, why everybody wants a car. It may be frustrating to sit in a traffic jam, but it at least doesn't make you feel an insulted no-body, as walking along in a main road does. Toby was pale with suppressed rage.

Down a quieter road. Houses getting fewer but still much distant noise. The low hills were just above us now, and when we walked off down a real country road with only two council houses in a field and some cows grazing in rough grass, everything began to feel different. I did wish it had been warmer.

"Bridlepath to Harefield", said a notice beside the road, with a pointing arrow, and there was a big gate all tied up with wire, so we had to climb over it and I laddered a stocking. This is no slight matter, in our circs., and though I only smiled silently at Mrs. Rode, it cast a gloom. There was also a lot of cow-stuff, and although the said bridlepath was raised above the corn growing on either side, it was lumpy and wettish, and it was so quiet everywhere. It got you down.

We had to walk in single file because there wasn't room, and Toby and Mr. Rode got ahead because they walked faster than Mrs. Rode and me, and when they turned to shout encouragingly to us we couldn't hear what they said because of the booming wind. The corn, which was still raw, swayed furiously on either side like a green sea. I did really hate it all, and my hair blew about. We were shut in by thick woods.

That bridlepath went on for what seemed miles. On we

stumbled, with aching ankles, and even Mrs. Rode seemed to be having less fun than usual. But she didn't grumble aloud or look sick. She is a nice woman. Even now, I still feel that.

At last we came to a thick green wood, damp and quiet, with silent birds darting about, and at least the path was softer.

"I am surprised by all this," said Mr. Rode, waving his hand at the trees, "so close to London."

Toby muttered something that I couldn't hear, and the wind shook the treetops. The trees went on for ages and then we came out into a big grass field, still shut in by those woods, and on the left was a high wall made of old red bricks. Trees were looking over the top.

Mr. Rode turned to us. "Hare House," he called, and made for a door that was painted a faded blue.

Heavens, that house was in a remote spot. It would have sent me quite mad to live in it.

We stood there, with the wind blowing all around us, and everything absolutely quiet, while Mr. Rode rang an old-fashioned bell that came out on a wire. The sky was low and full of hurrying grey clouds.

"Is he expecting us?" Toby asked, while we were waiting.

"Yes. These folk we met at the party are close friends of his, and they called him up and arranged everything yesterday afternoon. He said he'd have anything he knew about the Rodes written down for me," said Mr. Rode.

"He must be pretty lively, for ninety," said Toby.

"He is. They said he's a wonderful old gentleman."

But I was tired of oldies, and I was relieved when a man-servant-arrangement opened the blue door and told us that Mr. Cranford had died in the night.

I am sorry if I sound crude. But that walk, and the cool wind, and laddering my stocking and now being rather hungry, had put me into an un-pretending mood.

128

The old manservant looked sad : I think he had been crying, though of course oldies' eyes are often red naturally. He
said that Mr. Cranford had been expecting us, and almost the
last thing he did was to leave a note for Mr. Rode. The old
man said he would go and fetch it.

He asked us up to the house—I think Mr. Cranford must
have had kindly manners and trained his manservant to be
the same—but we said no, we wouldn't intrude. And as there
was not likely to be any hot food going, with someone frightfully old just dead, I was relieved again. Lunch would come
all the sooner.

Once more we stood waiting. We could see the house from
here, not glammed up at all, looking as if it had sat there for
a long time in a stodgy way, not wanting to be anywhere
else, or to look different.

It was made of plain red bricks, square and rather small,
with this big walled garden all round it, with positively
millions of scenty spring flowers.

I often think that you never know how lots of people live.
You think you do, because so many of them according to the
papers and the T.V. seem to live in the same kind of way.
But really, you don't.

Well, after ages the old man came slowly back and gave
Mr. Rode an envelope. When we had thanked him, and
assured him that he must not worry about our getting some
lunch (in the circumstances, he said, he was afraid that he
could not offer us luncheon), he retreated slowly behind the
blue door and shut it.

There we were, stuck up high on this ridge, with the
envelope in Mr. Rode's pocket book. It must have been nearly
two o'clock. And as Toby said, we had better not go on, as it
might land us miles from anywhere. What we had to do was
just to turn back and tramp along that track once more,
through those silent woods with unnatural birds flitting about

(you do expect a bird to be cheerful though perhaps I judge all birds by Aunt Edie's Willy) and over that bumpy grass again down the hill to Ware, by-passing Benfield.

When we got there it was three, and of course in every place people looked furious when we wanted lunch, except in a smelly café where we at last landed up where a notice outside simply said "SNACKS ALL DAY". As if the people who ran it knew that someone was bound to be hungry at any hour of the twenty-four, and had given up hope of running regular meal-hours.

XIV

Anyway, we had fried eggs and chips and tea, and very good they were, and Mrs. Rode smiled at the busmen and lorry drivers, who smiled back, in a grim sort of way. I was happy, having secured my g.h.m. for the day.

"Aren't you dying to see what's in the envelope?" I said to Mr. Rode, when we were smoking over our third cup of tea.

I felt Toby glance at me. He had not enjoyed the morning, for various reasons, among them being the fact that old dead Mr. Cranford hadn't been discovered by him, and he now thought that I was being nosy.

Mr. Rode smiled. "I have already satisfied my curiosity," and he handed me the envelope across the table.

"May I really?" I said.

"You really may. It only takes us on a little further."

Toby leant over my shoulder to read the sheet of paper, where the writing was old and shaky but clear.

"There was a Mrs. Thomas Rode, a widow with two sons, living in Water Street, Ware, when my father was a young man, in the nineties. She took in washing, as she was exceedingly poor, and the boys, who were wild rough lads, ran errands or held horses for a few coppers a time to earn a little money. At one time Mrs. Rode washed for our old friends the Carlyles, at Water House. The eldest boy went completely to the bad, went to London and incurred a series of sentences for petty theft. There is no trace of what became of him. The younger, William, seems to have at least partly reformed before he was thirty, and settled with a wife and family near St. Albans. He

131

started a small business in bicycles, when the fashion for them began, and went on to build it up and repair the first motor cars. But somehow he seems always to have kept up the family reputation for general shadiness.

"I hope that these scanty facts may be of use."

I found I was muttering the scanty facts over to myself, because I was so interested, but when I'd finished reading I didn't like to look up and meet the Rodes' eyes. 'General shadiness!' All very well, but these people *were* their ancestors.

"It's all right, Nancy," Mr. Rode said, laughing in his solemn way, "there are a number of qualities indicated on that sheet which I don't mind acknowledging. Grit, and enterprise, for example."

"Yes. We don't know, we just can't figure, what it was like to be so poor, and the temptations," Mrs. Rode put in. "Don't you love 'holding the horses' heads for a few coppers'? That makes it really come alive, for me."

"I wonder if the Carlyles still live at Water House?" said Toby—ready, I knew, to exchange taking in washing and holding horses' heads for something classier.

"We could stroll along and investigate." Mr. Rode got up from the table, and Toby paid our bill and we wended (that's a funny word, too) our way past the lorry drivers and bus conductors and out of the café.

A river called the Lea runs through Ware, and we soon found Water Street, which was a short street ending on the river bank. It had once been residential but now some of the big old houses were being torn down to build Council flats, and in the garden of one there were second-hand cars for sale and petrol pumps. There were also some little cottages, boarded up and deserted.

We found Water House, too. It was still elegant, as Mrs. Rode said, a large square white house with ironwork balconies at the windows and a garden running down to the river. But of course it was taken over by the Council now, you could see filing cabinets through the windows and girls sitting typing.

"So much for the Carlyles of Water House," muttered Toby, who hates to see private homes turned into offices. "I wonder where they are, and who does their washing now?"

Just then a van stopped near us with Pure White Laundry on it and I pointed at it and everybody laughed. This relieved the slight gloom caused by Toby's remark.

"Do you think it worth while just asking if anyone remembers a Mrs. Rode living here, sir?" Toby asked of Mr. Rode. "Or the wild rough lads?"

Mr. R. shook his head.

"No. I think not." He glanced from side to side at the street, with its look of being torn down and completely altered. "I don't see any sign of anyone living here who would know. Those little places"—we all looked at the boarded-up cottages —"that was where she would have lived, I guess, in one of those."

"They must have been empty for a long time."

"Yes."

My goodness, how I do dislike standing about in boring little Herts. towns looking at dreary places full of the past. I had had plenty of this with the Rodes, and while we were doing it the memory of delicious meals and delightful theatre-goings and the hope of more to come didn't make up for the excruciating boredom.

"Well, then. To St. Albans?" enquired Toby, looking ready to fly off. I know he shared my feelings.

"Not to-day, I guess. Bus to Benfield. I've got to get back. I'm seeing a man about buying an island."

This did rather stagger Toby and me. We did not dare look at each other. Oh, was it an island in warm seas, with palms and white sand? Mrs. Rode didn't make the situation seem more ordinary by murmuring in an excusing tone, as we walked back to the High Street, "It's quite a small one, really."

Mr. Rode did not follow this up. I got the impression that he did not want to talk about this island, and, for the first time since I had known them, I also felt, like something solid and touchable between us and them, the Rodes' money.

I knew that Toby, like myself, was wondering longingly whether we should be invited to visit them on the island? and we were both burning with curiosity. I was quite certain that it *was* warm, with coloured butterflies as big as birds. That was my picture, from the first moment we heard about it.

We were lucky with a bus to Benfield, and walked to the garage.

"Could you get us back as quickly as possible, Toby, I mustn't miss this man," was the only other thing Mr. Rode said in connection with the island, and Toby, more anxious than ever now to keep in with the Rodes, coaxed The Car so cleverly that in under the hour we were pulling up outside that tatty Chandos.

"Did you see—did you see?" Toby hissed, as we drove away.

"No—what—oh, isn't it thrilling—what?"

"A black face and a turban. Waiting inside the hall."

"Then it *is* a warm one! Oh, Toby!"

"Now don't let's get carried away. Perhaps it wasn't anybody for the Rodes at all. Highly unlikely he'd come in a turban, dripping sand over everybody, anyway. A lounge suit and a fez, yes. But it *was* a turban. Pink. I saw it."

"I wish, I *wish* we knew just *how* rich they are. It would help if we did, wouldn't it? How was the rest of him dressed?"

"I couldn't see. They keep that place so dark."

"Couldn't you just say casually the next time we see them, 'Did you get your island, sir?'"

"I might. But I think not. He's no fool. I used to think he was but now I'm not so sure, and—it's all very dicey. If I do mention it, it looks like impertinence—we don't know them well enough for friendly questions, you know—and if I don't, it *might* just look like playing cautious."

"Well we are, aren't we?"

"As much as we can, yes. But we don't want them suspecting."

"M-m-m——" I said, trying to make the noise sound thoughtful and constructive.

"What would be the *natural* thing to do?" I said, at last.

"Good heavens, Nancy, we don't want naturalness coming in yet! We aren't nearly far enough on with them for that."

"Sorry."

"All right. Only mind you remember it."

XV

WOULDN'T you expect that for the next few days Toby would talk of nothing but the island?

It only shows that you do not know his habits. By the next morning he had cooled off it, and was full of a plan cooked up by Randy Brookes.

Said that Randy's plan would at least provide a chance to meet some titles and earn a few guineas, while the island, so far as we were concerned, was more than probably a pipe dream.

His plan was related by Randy over the telephone, and its immediate effect on me was being sent out to buy a suit.

"You needn't spend the earth on it," said Toby, as he hung up the telephone, having spent some minutes getting instructions, "but be sure it's pink. Or yellow. Yellow, he says, would do. But pink is better. And it must look good."

"What's it in aid of, anyway?" I asked, not moving off the sofa, which was v. comfortable.

"He has to find some people to be the background for an advertisement—his firm has landed the contract for advertising this new cigarette, *Companion*—and he's putting in all his friends."

"Where do we come in?"

"A gang of us will drive out to some picturesque old pub and be photographed drinking outside it, using names—'the Hon. Lucy Lyon and Sir Willoughby Charters outside the Pig and Whistle at Church-In-The-Yard'—you know the line —and the copy will end up—'and they're smoking *Companions*.' You and me, too."

"What a mouthful of a name." I got off the sofa. A pink suit would be welcome. You have to either look very healthy all the time or paint very expertly, always to look well in black.

"And so? Jump to it, Idle. *Marche!*"

I went out with twelve pounds which would have to cover shoes as well. Toby said a hat would not be necessary, as he was aware that his views on hats were not shared by the great public. If my hair looked its best, that would do.

At John Barnes's I found a suit which I thought just right, and it was peach pink, which I have always liked better than rose, as being more sophisticated.

I was just coming out of the shop's main entrance when someone seized my arm and a loud well-known voice shouted —"Nancy! Where have you been hiding, all these months? Thought you must be dead!"

Even in this day and age, when the streets are swarming with Africans and so forth and characters straight out of *West Side Story*, people sometimes turned to look at Mrs. Raven.

She is very tall and very fat, with bright red curly hair and a huge face that has begun to slip downwards. Many people would try to disguise these disadvantages but Mrs. Raven wears the brightest possible colours and lots of jewellery. But above all it is her personality. Toby says she makes him want to run away and hide.

"Hullo—lovely to see you," I said in a warm tone—and it was true. Because she brought back my early youth, when all I had to worry about was whether I should see the good-looking paper-selling boy at the bus-stop, whom I exchanged back-chat with, on my way home from school. Happy days.

Also, with Mrs. R. I needn't be quite so on my guard as with Toby's friends. (This is a first-time confession, as no doubt you will notice.)

137

"You're looking very grand, dear. Married life going well? I bet it is!" and she threw back her head with a loud short laugh like an amused lion. "What's Toby doing these days? Settled down yet? Living in town, are you? Got yourself a job? I bet not, you always were a lazy little stinker." And she gave me a great push.

"Let's have a drink," I said. It was just on twelve, and I knew it was no use offering Mrs. R. coffee, which she scorned.

"Yo-ho-ho and a bottle of gin," she sang, not so loud as to sound as if she were tight, but loud enough to cause stares and smiles.

I did not like being called a lazy little stinker. I suppose being always with Toby *had* made me different, in some ways. Eight months ago, I would not have minded.

We found a somewhat plushy pub, and Mrs. Raven seemed to kind of expand, as she sat down at a table and quickly took a stare round the saloon bar. Most casual men in this kind of place always loved her, and I saw the sharp-faced barman relax into a smile as she caught his eye and winked. This was as I came up to order our gins and Cinzano. She let me carry them to the table, as if I had been her daughter—as indeed, she has always treated me. She does not get on with her own daughter.

Much depended on Mrs. Raven being clean. If she had been grubby she really would have been rather awful. I could see that, now. But she was not in the very tiniest degree grubby.

It was cheerful in that dim but sunny bar, with a group of men lunching early on stools, and drinking, and laughing. *How* I do like to see a group of men. So long as they are not consulting, or being drilled, or anything, it is a most promising sight.

Mrs. R. and I talked fast, exchanging all our news. One good thing about her is that she does listen, in spite of liking

138

to talk herself. She really is interested. I heard all about her boarding-house, which, of course, used to be my home.

"Your rooms are let to a couple out at business all day, nice people, she's a Belgian. They run a little sweets, tobacco and what-have-you but it's a lock-up. Shan't have them long, though, they've almost got their own place out at Edgware. And I've got four Indian students—one's a girl, going to be a doctor, got about a yard of black hair in a plait. There was a hoo-ha about curry at first, couldn't live without it, all right, I said, I'll learn to make your ruddy curry but only once a week, mind, all that fancywork with raisins, I haven't the time *or* the patience, but would you believe it, Miss Elliot and the Smiths—oh yes, they're still with me, and Miss Elliot's old aunt isn't dead *yet*, after all that fuss last year, so she still doesn't know if she's got the money—they all liked the curry so much it's curry three nights a week now. Doesn't work out too expensive, either, with cheap cuts cooked slowly and lashings of rice."

And so forth.

For a moment I felt homesick. I had been happy, in that huge shabby old house in one of those wide roads between Rosslyn Hill and Swiss Cottage, a sunny, warm place—Mrs. R. feared and hated the cold—full of cheerful noises and good smells. Mrs. Raven did herself well and everybody else too. All the people in dreary bed-sitters for roads round us looked wistful when you mentioned No. 14.

"Do you still have the Saturday nights?" I asked.

"Of course! Can you imagine Number Fourteen without the Saturdays? Shall I ever forget your father playing that drum? I've never laughed so much as I did that night—I often laugh, now, remembering it." Her little blue eyes, creased up in folds of pink fat, laughed at me over the rim of her glass as she spoke.

These Saturday nights were held in the basement. Any

boarder could come, and the only rule was that you brought a bottle and played on a home-made instrument. My father used to say this would have been agony for some people, but Mrs. R. did not have nervous or shy people at Number Fourteen. She could tell them at a glance and said all the rooms were full up. Nerves and shyness were the two things she could not stand.

Sometimes at the Nights we all played cards. If you didn't know how, Mrs. Raven would teach you.

In the middle of enjoying the talk and our drinks and the cheerful atmosphere it suddenly occurred to me to tell her about Guy. I had wanted someone worldly and kind. She was both.

Fortunately, just then she gave me a chance.

"But this is all about me. How about *you*?" she demanded, breaking off in the middle of telling about the Smiths and smiling more broadly at me. I got in instantly.

"I'm absolutely as happy with Toby as it's possible for a person to be," I said—hurrying over this sentence, for Mrs. R. is rather interested in some sides of being married—"but there is one thing I am worried about—" here her eyes gleamed, and I rushed on "—Toby's best friend is trying to get hold of me."

Straight out, I spoke. No delicate preparation, such as when I told Auntie Edie.

She gave a great laugh, throwing her head back so that her earrings wildly tilted.

"What, already? Well I'm not surprised. Always knew you'd have man-trouble. (If you can call it trouble.) Does Toby know?"

"Oh *no*, Mrs. Raven. That's what I'm worried about. Do you think I ought to tell him?"

"Tell him? Good Lord no, girl. You have your little bit of fun on the q.t.—don't do anything I wouldn't do, of course

—and, don't forget, new husbands are always very jealous."

"I don't want any fun," I said (really, I'd forgotten what Mrs. R. was like), "it's a question—you see, this is his best friend."

"Funny how often it is," Mrs. R. said, now beginning to look shrewd and kind of harder, "I s'pose they think that what suits their best friend will just suit them. Men!" She shook the earrings.

"I'm afraid of hurting Toby," I said. "If I tell him, I mean."

"Do him good!" she cried, "you don't want him thinking all the freedom's on his side. You can't break them in too young."

I said nothing but looked down at my gloves, lying on the table. It was plain that Mrs. Raven only knew about one kind of marriage, and I decided at once to ask her advice no more. Any that she gave me would be useless. I felt helpless again, and also a bit angry.

"Marriage isn't a kind of war," I said, in a light sort of voice, trying to turn the conversation.

"Oh, isn't it? That's just exactly what it is, and a damned good way of putting it too. It is 'a kind of war', and you're just too new at it to realize it, that's all. You take it from me, Nancy," she lent towards me across the table, "the sooner you let your Toby know you can attract other men and will, too, if he doesn't behave himself, the more chance you've got of your marriage lasting ten years. (If you want it to, that is.) Believe you me, I know what I'm talking about. I've learned the hard way."

I looked up and met the hard, yet kind, expression of her eyes. And I stopped feeling angry. She meant to be kind, she was only telling me what she thought was true. And perhaps, for her, it was true.

I picked up my bag and gloves. "Look, I'm afraid I must be getting along," I said.

"Now we've gone all haughty," cried Mrs. R., who does not like people to be getting along, even if the conversation has stopped being pleasant, "Well, I've said my say, and if you do tell him and there's an almighty explosion, don't blame me."

"I'm not haughty," I said, smiling at her. She was so much bigger than me that even when she was sitting and I was standing, our faces were almost level, "I'm very grateful for your advice."

"Oh the hell with grateful—it's a dirty word. If I can't give you a bit of help, at your age—why you aren't nineteen yet—with all *I* know about life, it's a poor lookout . . . how often I've said to myself, after the latest kick in the teeth from Fate or God or whatever you' like to call it, 'now, Doreen, what was the use of that one? What can you get out of it so's it won't be a dead loss.' And usually, d'you know, I can learn something."

She did not seem to have learned about some kinds of marriage, I thought. But, as I stood there looking at her big red drooping face, do you know what I was thinking? About the man in the Bible who, "passing through the waters of misery, used them for a well." One of the nuns used to quote it.

It was strange to think of Mrs. Raven doing that, yet she was, in a defiant, muddled kind of way.

I don't know what the kicks in the teeth were. I had always, until to-day, thought of her as being a perfectly happy cheerful character. Mr. R. was never mentioned of course, and as I have said she did not get on with her daughter, the one who bought my yellow frock with the diamanté clips. And very occasionally a boarder imposed upon her kind heart.

But I felt now that I must get back to Toby. (Although he often said that he and I belonged in the tiny percentage of people living in London who were free to keep their own hours, our life suddenly seemed rather restricted, to me, compared with life in the old days at Number Fourteen. Before I was married.)

Mrs. Raven put her arm round my shoulders as we went out through the swing doors.

"Don't mind me—I'm a bad-tempered old bag." She gave me a great squeeze. "Keep smiling, and no telling Toby—if you do, you can bet your best umbrella *you* won't come out of it snow-white, he'll be thinking you gave his friend the come-hither. Come in and see me soon. Bye-bye."

I said I would, and she gave me a final push and strode away, earrings swinging and shopping bag bumping into people.

It was *so* different, getting back to Toby. A kind of drop in temperature. But welcome.

"You have been drinking gin with Mrs. Raven," he said, after I had been in the room four minutes.

"Yes. I did meet her by chance in John Barnes's and we had a drink. How on earth did you know?"

"*Tiens!* You know my methods, Madame Maigret. Your breath smells of gin. Gin is a favourite tipple of Mrs. Raven's. Mrs. Raven lives near John Barnes's store. You have been to John Barnes's store. You have no other friends, so far as I know, who drink gin. Simple, chère confrère."

"There was no harm in it," I said. I was now sitting on his knee.

"None at all—so long as it doesn't become a habit. I won't ask how the old trout is. She always has energy enough for five, and she wearies me. No more of her. Let's see the suit."

He approved of it, and that afternoon I bought some white shoes he also approved, and I was able to give him two pounds change. That evening, the Rodes telephoned, and took us out to dinner and to see *Fiorello*. Dreamy.

143

I had now quite put all thoughts of telling Toby about Guy out of my head.

Two people as strongly different as Auntie Edie and Mrs. Raven had given me exactly opposite advice, and both kinds had been useless. So now I would drift along, and see what happened. Goodness knew, I was quite ready to.

The next day, Toby told me, we were to drive out to this place in Wiltshire to help make the photograph for Randy Brookes's agency.

And the next day was to be the most serious, so far, in all my life.

Thursday, the twenty-eighth of June, was the day darling Nancy grew up.

XVI

THE next morning was a fine day. I got up full of cheerfulness, and Toby and I had one of our laughing breakfasts, when we made the kind of joke, on and on and on, that is funny only to us because we love each other.

After breakfast I put on the new suit. It was neither pink nor orange but a delicate blend of the two colours. I also put on my white shoes, and an unusual amount of scent. (No blouse, it spoils the line.) I looked at myself in the mirror, and I looked very good, and I smelled delicious, and I stepped into The Car and sat down next to my Toby without a care in the world.

The first small cloud appeared when Toby announced that we were picking up Guy at Piccadilly Circus. I nearly said "Oh *no*," but managed to swallow it. Why did we have to have *him*? However, Toby would be there all day, so there was no danger of my being alone with Guy.

When we picked him up, he was wearing more aggressive motor-racing clothes than he usually does (because, I suppose, he had to look like one in the photo). I saw him give me a quick once-over, and he even made a comment.

Toby turned to smile at me as I sat in the back. He and Guy were arranging themselves in the front.

"Nancy's all right," he said. And I was. (But, you know, it was for the last time.)

"That pink is Randy's idea," Toby went on. "By the way, have you seen him lately?"

"Haven't seen him in weeks," said Guy.

"This advertisement-thing has got hold of him like some evil drug or something. He can't talk about anything else."

"Well it is his last chance. He's tried practically everything else. His family are beginning to kick."

"If anything goes wrong today with this photographing I expect him to lose his reason on the spot."

"Yes. Well, we shall see." Guy did not want to talk this morning.

Weeks afterwards, I remembered that this village we drove to was in Wiltshire.

I never knew its name. I think it appeared under the advertisement, when that came out, but I pushed the fashion mag. away when I did by chance come across it. Because all through that campaign for Companion cigarettes, the name on a hoarding or a bus or in the Underground gave me a sudden horrid pain in my stomach, and my heart beat faster.

Soon we were driving through a landscape dotted with large smooth green hills that looked ancient. The village we stopped at was quite unspoilt, and I heard Guy saying afterwards that it was purposely kept so by the inhabitants and local land-owners, because they could make money from time to time by letting tourist agencies and advert. firms photograph it. Guy said it was as good a reason as any, he supposed, for keeping a place unspoilt. Results were what counted.

Driving past houses and cottages of browny-grey stone, we stopped at last outside an old pub with a plant climbing all over it that Toby said was a fig. And indeed you could see the ripening fruit between the large leaves. The pub looked old and peaceful under the blue sky.

On the road near the village we had passed several cars with young characters in them, and now these came up at the same time as ourselves. Each carried, as well as various weedy young men, one girl, like a pearl in its shell, and I thought, suppose each one is an Honourable, or even a Lady? They would be irresistible to my Toby.

But these girls were not smashing as to looks. Their skins were good, but their voices loud and commanding and often their noses were large and their figures thick.

I felt less apprehensive. But the titles, of course, did remain.

There was Randy B. stalking among the chattering throng, telling everybody where to put themselves. Master of the situation. There were cameras, and technicians I suppose they were, and locals standing round grinning in rather a superior way as if they knew the pub and the figs and the trees would still be peacefully there when we had all driven away, and there was a terrifically important photographer in a yellow pullover that everyone called Freddy.

The weedy young men mostly wore those riding breeches which I cannot spell, the dictionary not giving the word. Everybody did look rather beautiful, being all young and well-dressed under a clear summer sky, and everybody was cheerful and friendly.

I must say that in spite of the loud voices most of those girls were rather sweet and dithery, and if they were Honourables or Ladys it didn't show.

Randy B.'s face is quite as large as Mrs. Raven's, though I would not upset Toby by saying so. He is a peculiar-seeming young man, sort of flabby, with limbs that do not seem to belong to him, and a suet-like complexion. Toby says he is extremely well-bred, and stays at all the country houses still functioning.

He ordered the girls about—"Vanessa, over here, ducky"— "Fiona, you go just there——" and so forth. Guiding them by the arm or the ear. I think he liked doing it.

This was Guy's Lady Vanessa, an earl's daughter. She was dressed in red, and was rather elderly.

Randy made Guy put The Car just to one side of the pub's big, comfortable-looking entrance.

"That do you?" called Guy, to the photographer **Freddy**.

"A wee bit more to the left—little more—just a fraction —that's it. Fab.! Oh, and now can you put her just quite not dead straight on? I want the sun on those gorgeous head-lamps, but not too much—no, that'll kill it—an inch back— that's right. Oh, perfect."

Freddy, who had been standing on a kind of oaken bench outside the door to direct the business, now hopped down, and a grinning groom led up a beautiful brown horse.

One of the girls roared, "Oh *there's* Monty! You got him safely here then, Phillips," and I was surprised to see the horse glance round at her. He did seem unusually intelligent.

"That animal is not to be brought within ten feet of me," said Freddy firmly, "yes, I know all you girls think I'm a shocking coward but I can't help it. That's the way I'm made. Take it away, George, please," to the groom. "Now, Hilary, up you go."

Hilary, the girl who had roared, was wearing riding clothes and a bowler hat. She now got up on to the horse, and sat there, looking, I must say, pretty. Randy and Freddy moved her over to The Car, so that Guy could lean out as if he were talking to her, and the rest of us they put in groups, just as if we had met by chance at the pub while out following the dogs or whatever it is people do in the country.

It did look attractive. Like a glimpse into an ideal life where everyone was young and rich and gay. Well that of course is what an advertisement does, makes you think that if *you* smoke the cigarette or use the detergent, you will feel like a Lady or a bright young housewife too. I think it a good idea, myself.

All day, or at least, for all the morning until **nearly three** o'clock, we were posed and re-arranged and had our photographs taken. Then we all went into the pub for a late lunch.

Now that pub was not homely and simple, but rather grand. People like the Rodes would stay there or drop in for a meal. And it had a small but unusually well-stocked bar, I heard Randy and Freddy commenting on it, and, although we all ate bread and cheese—because everyone protested at the prices—eighteen shillings for a three-course lunch! Imagine! —also we all drank a great deal. I did too, I am fond of drink, as you know, only not spirits so much.

Toby, I could see, was utterly happy. The socially O.K. surroundings, the titled people, and the carefree atmosphere, made him feel in his native air. From the first, I had noticed him hanging round the elderly Lady Vanessa, and as the afternoon went on they retired into a corner on a window seat, earnestly talking.

I knew that he only liked being with her because she was a Lady, so I did not much mind. And once or twice he did come over to see how I was doing, only to find me with Freddy's arm round my shoulders. Freddy said loudly that all his fancy dwelt on Nancy, and he was going to sing Tally-ho, and who was going to stop him? Then everyone sang Tally-ho.

Yes, it was quite a party, that one, and then, hours later, would you imagine it, Freddy and Randy dragged us all outside again to take more photographs. Randy was very solemn and made a speech about the importance of the photographs.

The evening air calmed everyone down slightly, and I think by this time we had all had enough, because people protested at the time that Freddy and Randy were taking, this time, to arrange the groups. It went on for hours—or seemed to.

By the time the last picture was taken, it was dusk.

And where was Toby? I looked around, and I could not see him anywhere.

Cars were being started up: the beautiful brown horse had been led away to a kind of large high van parked round the corner, voices were calling "goodbye", the technicians were packing up the cameras and Freddy was instructing them, in a cross tired voice, and where was Toby?

"It's no use, darling Nancy. This is it."

It was Guy, who had come up quietly and was standing beside me.

"Have you seen Toby?" I asked. I could not face it. The situation seemed too bad to be true.

"Toby, darling Nancy, has made off. Scarpered, skedaddled, vamoosed. (Odd, isn't it, how many words there are for running away?) In this case, with a girl not half as dishy as his wife. But of course there is the title."

I stared up at him. The soft dusk was just clear enough for me to see his smile.

"Don't be silly," I said, and then he seemed to pull himself together. He took my hand, and began to draw me gently towards The Car.

"It's all right, little one, he told me to tell you he's going to drive her home. She lives in Hertfordshire, he'll be home by midnight, he said."

Gloomy old Herts again.

"Why couldn't she drive herself home?" I said, my mind busy, now, with this difficult and dangerous situation.

"Doesn't like driving at night. And her boy friend had too much strong drink ge-taken."

I wished that Guy would for once talk in an ordinary way. I was used to the way that he and Toby talked, but now, with Toby off with this woman and knowing how Guy felt about me, I felt I just could not bear his queer slang. If only he would be ordinary and kind!

150

It *could* all have been quite ordinary. A little hurtful, but no more. It was Guy, with that look on his face that made everything seem frightening.

"Coming?" he asked, opening the door of The Car.

I hung back. "No, I'm staying the night here," I said, remembering even as I said it, that I had no money.

"Won't Toby think that rather peculiar? He did ask me to drive you back."

I was angry, and I'd had too much to drink, and I was beginning to be frightened of Guy, and now I suddenly felt like crying. Toby had remembered me. Even in the middle of revelling in his old Lady Vanessa's title, he had remembered me.

So I should ruddy well hope, I thought furiously. But I still wanted to cry.

Then, suddenly, I seemed to hear calm inner voices. They must of course have belonged to the ancestresses. (I must say that they do always come up with help when it is *really* needed.)

You must keep calm, Nancy Régine. This is no time for giving way, they said.

"Oh come along, darling Nancy. I give you my word I won't be violent."

"You said that before."

But I got into The Car and Guy shut the door after me. The evening was drawing in. The moon had risen over the dark trees, and locals were driving up to the ancient pub.

I caught a glimpse of Guy's face in the glare of the headlights as he went round to the driver's seat. It looked kind of reckless and bitter. But as he seated himself beside me, he said—

"One thing I do *not* want, please, is for you to think I've been drinking. I'm soberer than you are. Smell." He thrust his face so close to mine that I felt the warmth of it. And it was true. There was no scent of drink at all. I drew back, muttering something.

"So you don't have to be afraid for your skin." He started The Car, and she moved majestically forward.

"I got out of the habit of drinking, while I was driving," he went on. "I am going to talk to you, because it's time you heard what I've got to say. But please remember that I am *not* drunk."

"All right, Guy," I said mildly, "I can tell you aren't."

"That's all right, then."

For the next few minutes we didn't say anything. The Car quickly got out into absolutely open, still, country, along a dim white road, with towering shadowy trees. The moon was climbing higher every minute, and we passed from light into deepest shade with bewildering speed. Then out again, into the warm yellow glow. Except for the drowsy hum of the great engine, there wasn't a sound.

"Cold?" said Guy presently.

It was a very warm night. I think he only spoke to break the quiet, and to get started on what he had to say.

I shook my head and said, "Oh, no——" and then glanced at him. I had never seen such a look on any face. Reckless but absolutely determined.

XVII

"How much do you know about Toby?" He turned his eyes towards me, as he spoke, without moving his head, and it was queerly frightening.

I didn't answer. I remembered that he had asked me that once before, on that afternoon at the Tate. I thought, I'll wait, I won't say a word, until I see what his line is going to be. But my heart was beginning to beat unpleasantly.

"I suppose you think he is the son of Sir Austin Leland, with Lady South for an aunt, don't you?" Guy went on. "Well, he isn't. Old Toby's father was a solicitor, and not a particularly successful one, in Colchester. He died when Toby was thirteen. And Lady South has never heard of him."

He gave the wheel a touch, and we swung round a sharp curve and sped on, down another long, empty, moonlit road.

"So what do you think of that, darling Nancy?"

Still I didn't speak. Do you know, in some hidden part of of me, I think I had been expecting to hear something like this? It sounded unbelievable, I didn't believe it, and yet all sorts of tiny incidents that at the time I hadn't noticed now seemed to join together, and give me the feeling that it was true.

"Remember that day you and the Rodes went to Abbots-tower? She was there, it seems, and overheard him shooting a line. Remember him ringing me up that same night, and talking for hours?"

I did remember. And I remembered the look on my Toby's face, when I woke up and found him standing by the bed taking off his tie.

"My God, he was in a state that night. Kept asking me if he'd done anything against the law." Guy laughed sneeringly.

"The woman in the purple suit," I muttered.

"What? . . . he's so stupid, in some ways, our Toby, it isn't true. Against the law! The kind of thing a child of ten might have done. It took me nearly an hour to calm him down."

His tone was so crushing, and it made me feel so angry on behalf of Toby, that I had to speak. What I said was something I never meant to. I said it because it was uppermost in my mind.

"Don't you like him?"

That seemed to shake him. He said in a loud voice, "Of course I like him. Known him for fourteen years, haven't I? But I think he's a bloody fool, and I think you ought to know it. He lives in a kind of dream world. Could be dangerous, that, you know, if it were to spread to ideas about money."

"Well it hasn't so far," I said. As I had spoken once, I might as well go on. And I could hardly bear sitting there in silence, wondering what was coming next.

"Another thing——" Guy went on, as if I had said nothing —"He was at Bredecaister with me. That does happen to be true. But how do you suppose he got there—perhaps the most expensive school in England, with his father making eight hundred a year? Old St. Merryn paid for him."

His eyes slid round again and looked stealthily at me. I saw now that each time he was going to uncover some new thing about Toby, he did this. As if all the unkindness in him were looking slyly out at the world. Yet Guy wasn't really unkind.

"Mr. St. Merryn we met at the party?" I repeated stupidly —shock on shock!

"Mr. St. Merryn you met at the party. Very, very rich, very, very lonely, very, very—peculiar. Scraped acquaintance with Toby's mother because he had taken a very, very great fancy to Toby. Toby's father had been dead six weeks, Toby was going to have to leave the rotten little private school they'd just managed to keep him at, and God only knew what was to be done, Mrs. Leland didn't. And then—old St. Merryn and Bredecaister! You can't blame her, can you?"

"I don't blame her at all," I said.

At this, Guy looked right round at me, and laughed.

"She's a very, very far-seeing woman," he said, "and I'm *certain* she's never suspected a thing."

Of course, he meant that she had.

"I suppose you're hinting that Mr. St. Merryn is queer," I said, scorning to keep up pretences with him.

"Well, what do you think, darling Nancy?" He was laughing again.

"I think you don't believe it yourself," I said. "Why shouldn't he be a lonely rich man, afraid of women, or perhaps faithful to the memory of someone he'd loved and lost, who'd always wanted a son of his own?"

"And they all lived happily ever after," Guy almost shouted, throwing his head back.

"Sometimes people do, in spite of other people trying to prevent them. It mayn't be as white as I make it out," I said, "but I'll bet it isn't as black as you do. I shall ask Toby about it, anyway."

I saw him, out of the corner of *my* eye this time, give me a quick glance.

"*And* allowed him five hundred a year to play with. Not much, nowadays, but not to be despised by our Toby—since he was eighteen. Called The Reserve Fund, I believe."

I sat quiet now, thinking. My Toby. Oh, what lies—what a network, a wide, going-far-back, network of lies! And all I could feel was sorry for him. No anger, no indignation at being thus taken in. That's how it is when you truly love

155

someone. You lose the power to feel that they have done wrong. The nuns would say that this was a bad thing.

I only felt as if Toby were a little boy who had told marvellous stories about his toys, when really at home he had none at all.

I said firmly:

"Look here. I don't mind Toby not being Sir Austin Leland's son, why should I? I'm rather glad. I didn't like feeling his father scorned me, like someone in an ancient book, because my father was a journalist, and not a title. As for Mr. St. Merryn, Toby doesn't take money from him any more. He told me. About a month ago. At least——"

"I know, darling Nancy. They had one hell of a row. And why? do you think. Because Mr. St. M. felt that Toby was getting *too wrapped up in his wife*, and was behaving ungratefully. Hadn't been down to see him for weeks, and so on. So Toby walked out."

"There you are, you see," I said.

But I must admit this sounded black, being jealous of Toby's wife. However, I reminded myself that many people are jealous of people's wives, without necessarily being queer —Mothers-in-law, for instance.

Guy smiled. "I wonder just what he told you?"

"I'll tell you. He said Mr. St. Merryn was touchy, and he wouldn't be seeing him again because he wouldn't come in useful. And he said there wouldn't be any more Reserve Fund."

"Charming fellow, isn't he?"

I think that Guy now felt disappointed, because he had told me the worst, and here I was, seemingly not minding.

"Of course he puts me before that old man, however kind he's been to him," I said. "So I should hope."

"Darling Nancy, you're so smug," Guy sighed. The Car was swooshing majestically through some large country town, whose streets were sleeping in the mingled lights of street-lamp and moon. A few souls were about and a few cafés bravely open.

"All the same. Dropping the old man stone cold. If it hadn't been for St. Merryn Toby would be selling refrigerators," Guy said next.

I must confess that in the first confusion of getting my mind used to all this, I thought *that wouldn't kill him.*

But I controlled the thought. Toby selling anything I simply cannot imagine. It practically *would* kill him, and also he would be furious and the customers would see it. I did rather long to know why Mr. St. M. hadn't offered to have him trained to be a lawyer like his father. But I know nothing of such training, and there may be insuperable difficulties.

"How far are we from London?" I asked, having had enough of the swoosh of the engine, the moonlit silence, and Guy's spiteful revealings.

"About another hour. Sick of it? Shall I let her out?" You would think our conversation so far had been quite ordinary and cheerful.

"If you like."

I leant back, and felt The Car seem to stretch herself to the road ahead, while the note of the engine dropped to a thrilling, powerful hum. Guy's face took on a triumphant, smiling expression.

I could see, now how he must look when he was racing. I kept quiet, for heaven knew I had enough to think about.

But presently he began to talk again. And I realised that he was still trying to blacken Toby.

"You thought his mother was dead, I suppose?"

"Toby's mother? Isn't she?" (That slipped out. I was not quick-minded enough, really, to battle with Guy, and you must remember that I was on the defensive.)

"No. She's as good as, though. She lives in a bed-sitter in

157

Colchester on her old-age pension and something from some legal society, and a rotten little job in a pet shop."

I minded hearing that. I minded it more than anything Guy had said, so far. Making up lies about titles hurt nobody, but this was neglecting someone. I wanted to find out more, but I didn't want Guy to see that I minded. So I kept quiet.

"Toby does give her some money, from time to time."

I didn't say anything. I wondered whether he wrote to her or went down to see her, and I imagined her looking forward to seeing Toby, who makes everything seem brighter when he comes—and then him not coming. I expect he was all she had in this world.

It made me feel bad.

"Does she know about me?" I could not help asking.

Guy shrugged. "I don't know. Toby hardly ever mentions her."

He let that sink in, while we sped along for some time in silence. The moon was high overhead, and the little lights that had sparkled were all extinguished, except for a solitary one here and there. We were approaching a kind of faint glow on the horizon, however.

"Reading," said Guy. "Shan't be long now."

He sounded gloomy.

I expect he was. He had done a dirty trick, and it was added to his having tried to get hold of his best friend's wife. And it had had no effect.

Or so he thought. He didn't know how astounded and shaken I felt inwardly. Toby seemed a different person. Perhaps you do not know how frightening that can be?

Presently Guy said, in the most dreary voice:

"I oughtn't to have told you."

Well, really! For the first time I felt furious with him. I said, in a voice I tried to make as unkind as possible:

"It's too late now. You have told me. And you've been

disloyal to your best friend for nothing, because it makes just no difference to me at all. Absolutely not one single sausage. I shall forget it."

"I hope you can," Guy said, as if he really meant it, and he turned and looked miserably at me and I could see that his spiteful, evil mood had left him.

"You win," he said, in really an *awful* kind of voice; it made me think of Mrs. Raven saying one of the boarders had a face like Satan on washing day.

"Yes, I do," was all I said. Because now all I had to do was to keep him from knowing how nearly he had won.

He had made my Toby into a different person. Wasn't that nearly winning?

I loved him as much as ever—more, in a way, because now I was sorry for him, as if for the little boy who had no toys at home. But there was this secret between us, and the usual maddening complications you always get with secrets—you knowing and him not knowing you know, and so forth, so difficult even to write down.

And it was no use. No harm was done to anyone else, true, and I might pretend that I didn't mind, but I did mind. I minded him having lied to me.

Guy made only one more remark for the rest of that drive. Just as we were coming up the Finchley Road towards our turning, having driven for nearly an hour in absolute black silence, he muttered, "You going to tell him?"

I didn't want to speak to Guy or even look at him. I felt I might start to cry any minute, and if there is one thing I hate more than being sick, it is crying. I have cried only about twice, in my whole life since I left early childhood.

"All right. If anything happens, it's your fault," Guy said.

I think he was looking at me, but I didn't look at him. I got out, and slammed the door, and walked into Rowland

Mansions, and as I went up the stairs I think I heard him call, "Remember me."

But that was as the engine started. I heard it gather speed, and like a distant roll of thunder The Car passed away into the night.

XVIII

THE next thing I knew was Toby standing over the bed and saying in a queer disturbed voice—

"Nancy—Nancy. Wake up, darling," and shaking me.

I sat up, keeping my eyes half-shut against the brilliant morning light. I could just make out Toby's dim form in his dressing-gown. The wireless seemed to be blaring at the top of its voice.

"What on earth's the matter?" I said in a mumble, shaking the hair off my face.

"Darling, don't panic—there's some very bad news," said Toby, sitting down on the bed and gripping me in his arms. He was trembling. "It's Guy. He's terribly hurt. He was in a smash on the M.1 very early this morning—I've just heard it on the news. They say he's gravely—they——" and then Toby put his head into my neck and didn't say any more.

I expect you will think, after hearing the events of the former evening, that I kept calm, and was even secretly pleased?

Few people are as wicked as that. I expect even that former German dictator, Hitler, wouldn't have been. As for keeping calm, yes, I did, because the impulse to cry had passed off after a night's sleep, and I had to think what was best to do.

So I hugged and patted Toby, a little surprised to find that he felt the same as usual when I had thought of him as a different person, and presently he calmed down, and got up and darted across and snapped off the wireless, which was roaring about some strike somewhere.

The room seemed suddenly sunny and quiet.

I looked up at Toby, from where I sat in the bed and though yes, except for a grief-marked face, he *looks* just the same, too. Put *that* out of your mind, I thought; in these circumstances, with excuse for being worked up, something might get blurted out. Steady, Nancy Régine, the ancestresses advised.

"Poor, poor Guy," I said, and for the moment all I could think of was his face, and what he had said to me, as he drove away, "How awful for you, hearing it like that."

"Yes—I got up quietly, so as not to wake you, and turned the thing on and ran slap into it—turned it up to catch the end of it—didn't get the name of the hospital. I'll ring his firm—no, damn," glancing at the clock, "no one'll be in yet. What time did you get in, honey?" as if suddenly remembering me.

"About one." I was remembering that drive.

"Did he seem all right when you left him? I can't think what can have happened. Guy's famous, you know, for never having had a smash. We all had a lot to drink, I know. But he doesn't drink much, he's never got the habit."

"Oh no, he wasn't in the least drunk, when we left the village. He made me smell his breath."

Toby was looking in a distracted way first at the clock and then at the wireless.

"Couldn't you ring one of the newspapers? Hundreds of people will be, I expect," I suggested. "Or the B.B.C.?"

He nodded, and went into the next room and in a moment I heard him dialling.

I sat on the bed in the sunlight, feeling—if you must have the truth—*irritated*. I was an innocent party. I had not done one thing to make Guy get into a state about me. Yet here he was, smashed up in hospital, and the last thing he had said to me was, "If anything happens, it's your fault."

It was utterly unfair.

162

Suddenly I saw his face, as clearly as if he were in the room, and a great gulp came up into my throat and I seemed to melt inside, and I was crying. Really violently. I suppose all the feelings of yesterday had been collecting within me, and the news had triggered them off.

I heard Toby call from the next room—"Don't, darling—I'm coming—no, it's all right. Thank you. The Princess Anne Hospital, Luton——" and he rang off.

I mopped my face with my nightgown. You are a selfish *chienne*, I told myself. He's terribly injured, and here are you thinking about your hard luck.

I prayed.

I just managed to get one in before Toby came in, and hugged me up in his arms and rocked me and comforted me.

"They repeated the message. It was the *Express*. Grave injuries to head and back," he said. "Don't, darling."

On the wireless and in some T.V. plays and in women's magazines people always make coffee on these kind of occasions. I suppose it does good to some people, especially if they've been sweating things out. Others are reminded of the small comforts lying beyond this awful hour. *When it's all over* . . . they think. Not knowing that things will never be the same again. They just don't know.

But I do so hate being unhappy. My heart kind-of turns to happiness, like a child to a bag of sweets. It was no use calling myself a *chienne*, I did resent it all.

Toby and I didn't make coffee. We each had a strong, strong drink, and sat on our bed, holding each other.

"Hell," Toby remarked presently in an absent voice, "we're supposed to go hunting with Clay and Maybelle to-day."

"They won't expect us to, surely? Won't they have heard?" I said, and then the telephone rang.

Toby put me gently aside and went to answer it, and at once I heard that it was Mr. Rode.

"Yes—I don't know, sir, I haven't any later news—I was just going to call the hospital—oh, you have? No change. Well, I suppose that's better than . . . no, I hadn't thought of going. They'll have let his sister know, of course. She'll probably fly down from Scotland this morning." Then a pause, as if Mr. Rode were talking. Then Toby said, in a more normal voice,

"Right. Yes, I agree. Nothing worse than hanging about. Oh that'll be all right, I can hire one. At twelve then, at the Chandos."

I must admit that I felt nowhere could be worse to be, at such a time, than the Chandos. But I told myself to stop it. If we had gone to the Caprice, the thought of Guy would have been there, underneath the cheerfulness and gaiety.

Toby, I knew, also minded very much about The Car. He had driven her so much that he felt he had a large share in her, and as we drove to the Chandos in an ordinary hired one he told me that he and Guy had always called her his mistress.

"Guy's wife, my mistress," he said. "I haven't asked about her—well, there wasn't anyone to ask, and anyway it would have sounded utterly peculiar. We'll get a lunch edition—they're just out."

He stopped, and we got a *Standard*, and there on the front page between Cuba and some girl flying in was a picture of The Car.

You never saw such a pile up. Nothing could be seen clearly but twisted machinery and an impression of great ruin. You felt that none of it would ever move again. It was all sideways and jammed together. But you could just distinguish The Car's headlamps.

"*God*," said Toby, staring.

"It does look awful," I said faintly, thinking of Guy being pulled out of that.

"But what was he *doing*?" exploded Toby, and I knew he

164

felt so bad that he had to get angry to let it out. "There must be four cars there, it looks like a rail smash. If he wasn't drunk, what was he doing?"

I didn't say anything. I could have said something like, *remember how fast The Car could go, perhaps he couldn't resist the empty M.1 stretching away in the small hours and got careless, perhaps he was slightly drunk after all.*

But I resisted. In a muddled way, I felt I mustn't say anything to hint that Guy might have done it on purpose. That would be the absolute end.

I didn't in my heart feel that he had. My common sense told me that he hadn't done anything so bad, after all, only given away his best friend's mild deception.

No, I didn't feel that had upset him. I had a dreadful feeling that he *really* did love me, and he felt guilty because I was Toby's wife, and felt he oughtn't to have told me he loved me, and—at last he knew I didn't love him. And it was *that* that had strained his nerves and made him less careful in driving than usual.

Perhaps, for a few seconds of utter depression such as come to many seemingly gay and successful people, he had wondered what life was all about? And in those seconds his eye and his hand were off guard, and it happened.

That was the thought that was now in my heart and would never go away again. That was what I meant when I said Nancy darling finally grew up. Because one of the chief signs of being grown up is bearing painful secrets in silence so as not to hurt other people.

Toby crumpled the paper and put it on the seat.

"This kind of thing makes you as sick as muck with everything else, doesn't it," he said, starting the boring hired car. "I suppose we'd better get going."

In spite of my painful thoughts, I must admit I had once or twice wondered if I was going to be told what had happened with Lady Vanessa. What time he had got home, and so forth, because he hadn't been back when I got in on the previous night.

But evidently I was not to be told yet. And if it had all gone out of his head under this unexpected news, probably nothing of importance had happened.

Lunch was of course the most worried, serious occasion you can imagine. Mr. and Mrs. Rode made no attempt to hide their concern. Though they did not talk about the situation itself, their feelings showed in continual talk about Guy—his kindness, his likeableness, amusing things he had done or said, how much their dead son, Bill, had liked him, and so forth. We laughed shortly at some of the amusing things.

As usual in such circumstances, the question of eating presented itself—wasn't it inhuman to eat a good lunch when Guy might be dying and so forth, and oh well what good would it do him to go without? All going on inwardly—in me, at least. Toby never eats much and quite small things put him right off, and the Rodes, I had noticed from the beginning, were always unusually small eaters. How I do *hate* anxiety and grief.

After lunch Mr. Rode and Toby decided to telephone the hospital again. There was no change. We bought another paper, and it had a lot about Guy's past, as if he were dead already, and how he had been great friends last year with a girl named Viola Casti, who Toby said was every 'rich boy's tart'. There was a picture of Viola Casti in a white fur coat, and apparently she had been telephoning the hospital every hour.

Toby said he wasn't surprised to see *her* cashing in. I was a bit shaken by this fabulous girl, and felt I had perhaps been making an unnecessary fuss about Guy's trying to get me. Though of course he might have dropped Viola Casti, as he had Lady Vanessa.

Anyway, that was all over now. All that mattered was,

166

would he die? The papers and wireless were already asking that, in concealed ways.

After all, we did hang about, though it was in the hired car and took the form of cruising sadly round the summer lanes outside Luton. I think Toby wanted to be near his friend.

I felt awfully tired. I suppose it was feeling so much for such a long time. We didn't try any ancestor-hunting that day, it seemed unimportant.

We bought another paper at tea-time and it said Guy's sister, Miss Lucy Murray, had flown down from Scotland, as Toby had thought she would, and there was a lot more about Viola Casti, who was still telephoning the hospital every hour though she was in Miami, and I couldn't help saying it must be costing her a fortune and Toby said *she* wouldn't be paying.

I was surprised to find how well known Guy was. I think people also liked him.

It seems hard when someone cannot die in peace. But Guy was a strong cheerful person and publicity is useful when you are a racing motorist and I expect he would have welcomed it. But I kept having an inward picture of him lying covered in bandages and all this somehow having nothing to do with him. Nothing. The papers, and the wireless bulletins, and Viola Casti, and all the fuss. Nothing.

I caught myself wishing *something* definite would happen.

That evening I also longed to go out somewhere to take my mind off it, and I really thanked Providence when the Rodes said we must all go to a show. So we went to *Beyond the Fringe* which I liked fairly well only I could not give my mind to it, and when we came out of the theatre Toby snatched a paper from a man selling them at the corner.

We all knew, as we stood round while he held up the paper to look, what we were going to hear.

A few days later a note came from Guy's sister.

It just said that she knew Toby would want to hear Guy had died peacefully, while he was unconscious. But earlier, in the afternoon, she added, he had been conscious for a few minutes, and he had known her, and spoken to her, and even mentioned us. He had said "Give my love to the Lelands". He had repeated it, she said—"Give my love to them both."

Toby went to the funeral. But I said I could not bear it, and he understood.

And oh, I was thankful, *so thankful*, that I had never told him.

XIX

I WROTE *things will never be the same again.*

It is true, but not utterly true. Outward things do go on as usual. But when you know something that makes the person who is closest to you seem a different person, and when someone like Guy has died, it is so strange to do and feel the things that you did and felt before the change came. It is the ordinary things in life that feel different.

For the next few days after the funeral Toby left me alone rather a lot.

He is secretive. I expect you have noticed that. He doesn't like showing me when he is miserable or worried. (I shall have to work on this. I am the wife, and she is there to share the burdens. Also, I like to know what's going on.)

He grieved for Guy by himself, or perhaps sometimes in silent drinking with Randy.

I talked to Randy once on the 'phone during those days. There was nothing secret about *his* grieving. He kept on for ages, saying the same things over and over again. I think he really was fond of Guy.

But mostly I was alone.

I got to hate that flat. The orrery particularly got on my nerves. It seemed so useless—stuck up there, good for nothing, when the electric iron had gone wrong, and we couldn't have it repaired because Toby said we were short of money. I did try to live at the cinema, but money came in again there.

I asked Toby once what the Rodes were doing, and he said oh, they were all tied up with this island, some people were lucky, having nothing to worry about except deciding which island to buy. So I said no more.

Toby sorrowed terribly for Guy, I am sure, missing him, but I think he also worried, in a more practical way.

Right at the beginning of this large mass of writing, you may remember I quoted Toby saying "My God, we're lucky to have Guy," and though at that time I was jealous of Guy and thought that we could have got on well enough without him, I now began to see how much we had depended on him.

You see, Guy knew just the kind of people Toby wanted to know, who lived the kind of life he wanted us to live. Rich enough to be generous with free meals and week-ends and trips, but also slightly—not exactly shady and illegal but—*carefree*.

We had met the Rodes and Randy Brookes through Guy, remember, and Lady Vanessa. (I suppose I must count her, as well.) To say nothing of the unknown character whose flat we had borrowed.

(Though all news of the slightly elderly Lady Vanessa had ceased since the day of Randy Brookes's advertising stunt, and I hoped all thoughts of her and phonings or writing or meeting had ceased as well.) All we heard of her was a reference in some paper to her having been a friend of Guy's.

Guy had *liked* us. These people we met through him— they were carelessly lavish with their advantages, but so they were to everyone, and at any moment someone might cut in under our noses and get the meals and the trips and shows. Guy had really had our welfare at heart. He had seen to it that, whenever possible, we got in first.

I still wasn't sure if the Rodes liked us in that way.

They were charming and generous but not in the way of Guy and his friends, it was in a more *distant* way, and our conversations with them were about 'having fun' and details in the past lives of the ancestors, or else huge questions like war, and social changes, and the under-privileged. (Money was never seriously mentioned.)

After the funeral, to which they went, they left us alone for five days.

Toby got in a state. Said they had dropped us. My advice that he should 'phone them he scorned, saying if they wanted us they could come to us. Our monthly cheque was due in a week, and then perhaps we should know.

But, he said, how were we going to get to know *new* rich and useful people? (He didn't say *now Guy is dead* but I knew that was what he meant.) Because we both knew, in our hearts, that *"Oh, they're friends of Guy's"* had been a password for us.

"They were friends of Guy Murray's" wouldn't have at all the same effect. People forget so quickly.

Toby worried and away most of the days and evenings, Guy dead, and us short of money. A dreary, lonely time.

I had to fall back on occasional coffee with the local oldies, whom you may have almost forgotten. And in connection with them, something really splendid now happened.

One evening I had the wireless on to listen to Helen Shapiro, just before six o'clock. I was twiddling the thing about to make it louder, and in the middle of a song, there was a ring at our bell.

I trailed out to answer it, and when I opened the door there was a crowd outside—Miss de Havilland, Mr. Pegram, old Mr. Haynes (the retired solicitor who lived alone amid the empty flats on the ground floor) and three or four other oldies, unknown to me.

They were all brandishing (another unusual word) wine glasses and looking madly cheerful.

"Ha! She's at home! Splendid," almost shouted Mr. Pegram. "Come along, Mrs. Leland, we're celebrating."

"Yes, come on, downstairs. To Mrs. Rawlings's flat. Come along!" they all cried, beaming kindly among their wrinkles and grey hair and spectacles. "Come along, Nancy," Miss de Havilland said.

"Yes, Nancy. Why not? Sweet name," said Mr. Pegram. (Getting reckless, you see.)

I was awfully pleased. The sight of all their cheerful faces cheered me.

"What's happened?" I asked, pulling my front door after me but not shutting it and following them down the stairs. "What are you celebrating?"

"Rhoda—Mrs. Rawlings—has won two hundred and twenty thousand pounds," excitedly said a very old one in a plastic mac and a faded headscarf. "*Two hundred and twenty thousand pounds*, just fancy. On the Pools."

"Oh, how *splendid*," I exclaimed, as we all surged (tottered, rather for some of them) up to Mrs. Rawlings's open door. "How *absolutely gorgeous*."

And when I saw Mrs. R. standing in the middle of her dusty old books presiding over an enormous—but a truly colossal—bottle of champagne and a fleet of dimly glittering ancient glasses arranged on the table among the racing papers, and beaming calmly on us all, I was so absolutely delighted that I went up to her and hugged her.

"Congratulations," I said. "It's wonderful."

"Thank you, dear child," and she gave me a hearty kiss, "will you prop the door open, Alicia, my dear, I think Mrs. Seymour and Mr. Wilbur are coming up later, and Miss Eliot, from Saint Anne's. Thank you. Now, Alfred," to Mr. Pegram, will you open the champagne." Alfred bustled up to the table.

"This is really delightful," said Miss de Havilland, smiling round on the smiling faces and the books and the dust and the bunches of roses, pink and yellow and white, arranged in saucepans and old Chinese vases, "I haven't seen a double

magnum since that last party at our Embassy in Bucharest—
in July 1914, was it?"

The cork came out with a mellow musical pop, and the
creaming foam! Mr. Pegram and Mr. Haynes managed it
beautifully. You could not say that none was spilled, but
that only added to the gaiety. The sparkling drops splashed
on to the dusty table, and I heard another old thing saying
they were *fairy footprints*. Old people seem to be completely
different from normal people. Fairy footprints!

But oh, I did enjoy that party. Coming on top of the
sadness and loneliness of the past week. More old things came
creeping in, peering and smiling, one or two of them with a
little dog which added to the gay confusion (though as you
know I am not fond of dogs and also Snowy de Havilland
came, though only to sit on the mantlepiece looking hatingly
at everybody.

There were many plates of delicious *petits fours* and
canapés, and I heard someone saying Mr. Haynes and Mr.
Pegram had been down in a taxi to Fortnums, and Berry
Brothers in James Street, W. (which is a very grand wine shop)
to buy everything, and bring it home. Mrs. Rawlings stayed
behind, polishing a few glasses before she got quite lost in a
book she was reading that was lying open on the table, called
Talks with Elementals.

She did take it all calmly. While she was telling me about
it, with her eyes looking more than ever like greengages
behind her Billy Bunter spectacles and wisps of hair floating
unheeded, I thought how Toby and I would have behaved.
Wild, crazy, delirious with excitement, even fainting, perhaps, from shock and joy.

I was just looking at her and having these thoughts when
I heard Toby's voice. "Yoo-hoo! Nancy!" and there was his
young face in the doorway, looking like sunlight among all
those old ones. He was holding up a letter and smilingly

nodding. Oh goody, our cheque had come, so we were not dropped.

"What are your plans, Mrs. Rawlings?" said Toby, when he had been given a drink and a whole plate of canapés by Miss de Havilland who I think was tight (no wonder—unlimited champagne, and over ninety.

I knew he must be seething with, well, jealousy. Mrs. R. was so old, perhaps having only ten or more years to live, and most of his life and mine was yet before us.

"Ah, yes, plans," Mrs. Rawlings answered placidly, "well, I have long thought what I would do if ever I won a really large sum, of course."

"Don't we all," smiled and nodded my Toby. I admired him. Not a sign, not the smallest hint, of envy.

"Yes. Well, I shall offer to buy this building from the new owners."

"Oh, jolly good. And will you stay on here?"

"Oh yes. My friends, all the remaining tenants, can pay me a nominal rent, and I shall offer flats at a lower rent to friends round about who lack privacy and comfort."

"It's a wonderful idea," Toby said heartily, "after all, that's the best of a windfall like this—you really can do things for other people."

Mrs. Rawlings looked at him silently. I wished I had been able to warn him beforehand that she was far from being as dotty as she seemed.

"Yes," she said, with a faint sigh.

"Do you have a system or was it just luck? I mean, do you really—are you at all interested in football?" Toby was a little drunk, like the rest of us, now, and I could see that he simply could not leave the subject. It fascinated him.

"I am interested in anything that makes human creatures more alive."

It was peculiar, while Mrs. R. was talking about buying

174

Rowland Mansions, she had seemed businesslike and ordinary, if calmer than most people would have been. Now, however, you were suddenly aware how greengagey her eyes were. The Rays coming up any moment now, I thought.

Toby laughed rather sillily. "Oh yes. Yes. Do tell me, you're keen on the Occult, aren't you, poltergeists and that kind of thing, did it help you to win? I mean, did you use occult powers?"

That'd done it, I thought.

I wished I could have pulled his coat or poked him. He didn't understand and I was embarrassed for him.

"Oh no. Never," Mrs. Rawlings said in a kind of calm, *gliding*, but extremely firm, tone. "The Rays do not come through to our sphere for that kind of work. Their work is Love, the implanting, nourishing and reaping of Love. In fact, had I attempted to use them for such an impure purpose as working out Pools, the results would probably have been strongly negative. It has been known."

"Has it," murmured Toby, whose eyes were getting glassy. (I suppose he'd had no lunch.) Mrs. R. continuing to look at him not at all crossly, added, "They are not like electricity, you know, to be generated and switched off at human will."

I could see that Toby had lost interest in The Rays. "I say," he said, in the kind of tone that is meant to stir up the excitement again (quite unnecessary, because all the oldies were talking, drinking and laughing more than ever), "you must make a speech."

"Oh no. Unnecessary." Mrs. Rawlings shook her head.

"Oh, come on! Speech, speech," and he began banging on a dusty little occasional table. One or two people glanced round, surprised and smiling, but only the old thing in the plastic mac took up the cry.

Mr. Haynes came up to us.

"Mrs. Rawlings has been suffering from slight laryngitis, I

175

think it's unadvisable——" he said, and as the lone cries of Plastic Mac ceased at that moment, the whole thing died away.

"I shall tell my friends individually," Mrs. Rawlings said, looking peacefully round on the happy throng.

"Don't they know yet?" said Toby—much struck, I could see. Why, all this goodwill and rejoicing was utterly on behalf of Mrs. R.! They didn't know, yet, how strongly they would all benefit.

"Mr. Haynes is going to draw up a contract," said Mrs. Rawlings, and I saw Toby look quickly at the old gentleman.

"We have agreed that they would prefer it," Mr. Haynes said. "I have been Mrs. Rawlings's solicitor for years, indeed, it was through her recommendation that my dear wife and I came to Rowland Mansions, and I know every detail of the situation."

At the word "solicitor", I happened to catch Toby's eye.

I couldn't help it, I think my knowledge and anxiety were all showing in my face, because we exchanged a long look, quite different from our usual loving one.

I couldn't read Toby's expression. I only know that it was not so *shattered* as I would have expected. Relief? It *couldn't* be relief.

At this moment Plastic Mac tottered up, still looking dashed. (Well, I have never shouted alone in public, but I can imagine how it feels.)

"I must go, Rhoda—yes, yes, I must, really, Kitty will want her supper." It was plain that poor Plastic Mac was wanting to show remorse.

"Must you, Hester? Oh, do stay. Or won't you go home and fetch Kitty? Snowy de Havilland would love to meet her. Yes, do that."

I was now dreading, yet wanting, to be alone with Toby. Since that queer long, long look, he had not said a word, but

176

stood quietly, turning the wine round in his glass and watching it swirl.

I said good-bye and thank you for a lovely party and once more congratulations, while Mrs. Rawlings was still persuading Plastic Mac to come back with Kitty and make a night of it, and then Toby and I, saying good-byes as we went, made our way through the crowd and through the door. Mrs. Rawlings had not asked us to stay.

I would not be surprised if those Rays had told her that something important was going on between us.

XX

WHEN we reached our own landing, Toby stopped.

"How long have you known?" he asked, and then, before I could say anything, "Guy told you, I suppose?" He did not look at me as he spoke.

For a moment, I did not know what to say.

"Oh—some time now," I said, coolly lying, because the only thing was to keep him from being hurt, and maintain his pride.

He didn't say anything for a moment, while we were entering the flat, and then he said:

"There was no harm in it."

"Of course not, angel."

"Guy always did say it was childish. But why did he tell you, I wonder?"

Help me, ancestresses, I inwardly begged. And, of course, they did.

"I think he was worried about you," I said, choosing words, but not obviously. "He thought you might get carried away by it and perhaps get in some bad jam about—money."

"*He* always was fond of money," said Toby with a strong sigh, collapsing into a chair and putting his arms behind his head (a good sign. He was going to talk.) "Funny thing, the only dirty thing I've ever known old Guy suggest was over making money."

I didn't say anything, only looked quietly interested. Toby was drawn and pale. My Toby. I loved him so much. I felt as if I were treading a way through broken glass.

"Guy had some shares in the company that bought these

flats, you know," Toby went on, "and what's really been holding them up and preventing their getting all the tenants out is old Pegram. His great-grandfather built the place, and he's always had a 'gentleman's agreement' about his flat. He was to live there rent free, no matter how often the building changed hands. This new lot aren't gentlemen," Toby said with light bitterness, "except for old Guy and the one you call Oriel-Man, and oddly enough it was one of the two gents. in the setup who made the suggestion to *me*—who had only pretended to be a gent."

"What suggestion, darling?" I went over and sat beside him in the large chair.

He had at last put me ahead of Guy, not on a level. Guy was dead, and he was condemning Guy to me, and I was *first*. I was so glad. Now I was *truly* the wife, absolutely first in Toby's heart.

"Oh, nothing so very vile. Just sucking up to the old man, and working on his feelings and persuading him to clear out. Guy said Pegram had taken a fancy to me. Perhaps he had. I don't know. But I must admit his suggesting that gave me a nasty jar. I couldn't understand it. Guy's people weren't stinking rich, of course, but his family had always had position. He was completely sure of himself. Wherever he was or whatever he did was all right, because *he* was all right. Didn't he give you that feeling?"

I thought it best just to nod.

"I was romantic about Guy's family, you know," Toby went on, putting his arm round me and resting his head on me. "It seemed to me a marvellous thing to have an ancestral home in Scotland, family traditions, and portraits, and documents, and all that. And ideals. (I took the ideals for granted.) So . . . it did shake me when he suggested I should sweeten old Pegram."

179

"It was peculiar, I think," I said, carefully not using a stronger word.

"I felt he'd only asked me, you see, because I wasn't really a gent.," Toby said, looking at me and speaking defiantly, "at least, not in the sense that Guy was."

"Now that really is crazy," I said, this time with firmness, "if some of the others were gents., why didn't he ask one of them, instead?"

Toby sighed. "Oh, I don't know. He always thought I was soft, I think. (He used to say the one thing you dared not be in the modern world was soft.) But, you see, I was at perhaps the most expensive Public School in England, Nancy, and there are just some things a Public School man doesn't do."

Having met this man before, and not thinking much of him because he struck me as not being a real person at all, I spoke even more firmly.

"Well, Guy was there, too, and he did them. Or he wanted you to do them, which is worse. Don't you think all kinds of people don't do some things, not only Public School men?"

"I suppose so," sighing, "I don't know." He kissed the top of my head. "I know my life is very difficult, but thank God I've got you. I'm hungry. Let's go out to dinner."

So we went, and the evening ended quite cheerfully.

I think Toby was relieved to share some of his secrets with me. We didn't discuss it any more. He could feel, I expect, that it was him I loved, not his supposed connection with Lady South and Sir Austin, and, because I loved just him, I was not going to mind having been lied to.

We had heavenly duck for dinner. How very much more satisfying real things are than ideas, or thoughts, or feelings.

.   .   .

The Rodes enclosed a note with their cheque. It referred among other things to the island.

180

From now onwards, this island is going to grow larger and larger.

First of all, it was no more than a word, with a kind of dim fringe of warmth, and blueness, and palms, surrounding it. Then gradually, as summer in England went on, crowded and noisy and not very hot; and Toby and I were feeling older and sadder because of the death of Guy and other happenings, the Rodes began to show signs that it was growing larger in their minds, and so it began, as it were, to loom out of the sea, with low purple mountains and white beaches, and sweet scents, and laughing brown natives.

But with some solid buildings, of course. I never have liked the idea of those little huts, which blow away as soon as there is a typhoon.

They never described it to us, or mentioned it except casually, and we were both slightly annoyed by this. It seemed to shut us out from the more interesting part of their lives. Gloomy old Herts., we felt, smelling of chips and over-run by lorries was good enough for the Lelands. (Not that I scorn chips.) "When we get to the island," the Rodes some-times said, exchanging smiles, or "that will depend on the island."

I sometimes wondered if it was real.

Then, one day about a week after Toby had talked as described, the island got itself a name, and from now on I shall either give it a capital letter, like this, The Island, or its name, which is, in English, The Place of Many Palms.

The Place of Many Palms. Could anything sound more romantic and desirable?

From the moment I heard this name, a glow of warm moonlight seemed to shine out from the place. I always saw it by night, starred and hushed, with the languid breeze sigh-ing through one of those lofty airy shelters they have in those countries, raised on pillars made of dark wood and decorated with mother-of-pearl.

Apparently, though, there was much complex business involved in buying it, and also we could not find it on any map.

"Too small," said Toby, as we pored over atlases in the Public Library, "just big enough for the four of us and a household of devoted native servants."

"Living in little huts round the big house."

"Bringing us iced drinks at sunset wearing fresh wreaths of flowers."

"Padding with shining bare feet on the shining wood floors— —"

"Sticking flowers in their hair to— —"

"Singing— —"

"Diving into those very green pools— —"

"All in glorious Technicolor," we said together, bursting out laughing.

But such places are real, you know. They do exist. Perhaps not quite as they do on Cinerama, but they are there. If it comes to that, I suppose there are still hushed places that smell fresh in gloomy old Herts.

But not warm. Oh, not warm. And as the weeks went on we began to think more and more about The Island, and to hope wildly that the Rodes might invite us to go there with them.

I think this hope grew stronger as the summer drew on to August and no prospects turned up for us. Randy Brookes, Toby told me, seemed to have dropped him, not on purpose, probably, but just because he was busy as usual with one of his crazy schemes and also because he would never think of us as he did of Guy. "Guy *belonged*, you see," Toby said, in the most bitter, hopeless voice.

It really was all a lot of rubbish and nonsense.

I felt this more as time went on and I saw how Toby felt

about titles and birth and all the rest of it. You can find warm, brave, likeable people anywhere, but my poor Toby thought that only titles and so forth were worth having.

It was a kind of delusion.

Anyway, though all this about Guy's death and Mrs. Rawlings winning the Pools and Toby and me having our talk about his deceptions has taken some time to tell, really it all happened in less than three weeks, and the letter from the Rodes which Toby brought to that party contained a plan for our all meeting to follow up the clue given by that old man who had died in that remote house.

You will be wondering about The Car. How Toby managed after it was smashed up, I mean, as the Rodes thought that it had belonged to him.

But you see they hadn't thought so, for some time. Fairly early on, Guy and Toby leaked the info. out to them one day when we were all at lunch, and it went off very well, Mr. Rode teasing Toby about pretending to own it and saying Toby and Guy were The Firm and so forth and not minding, apparently, in the least.

Even said, in the letter, that a smaller car might be more useful for going down narrow lanes. That was kind. He meant that Toby needn't spend money on hiring something gorgeous.

So one stuffy August morning, there we were driving down to the ancient Chandos again, as if nothing—Guy's death, Toby's confession—had happened.

"Think I might pump him a bit about The Island to-day?" Toby asked. (I noticed that he had taken to seeking my advice lately. I liked this, of course. The wife should be consulted.)

"Well if you do, be careful. I can't help feeling that if they'd wanted us in on it, they'd have told us more, by now."

"Yes, it is rather treating us like servants," Toby bitterly said.

I nearly said well, if you base your life on worming in with rich people, that's how you will be treated, unless you're mighty lucky. But of course I didn't. It was a disloyal thought. I had been having those, lately. It wasn't that I wanted the little house and Toby in a nine-to-sixer, and the baby. But I didn't like depending for our comforts on sweetening people, and trying to manoeuvre them.

It was a *bore*. Toby might enjoy it but I kept on forgetting what to say and do.

"Well," Toby said as we stopped outside that dreary old place, "to-day I'm going to have a stab at it."

XXI

THE Rodes looked the same as usual. Mrs. R. had a corny new hat, but she was always having corny new hats.

"St. Albans, isn't it, sir?" Toby asked, as we drove up Regent Street. I think we had all been remembering The Car (on some scrapheap now, perhaps) and Guy, though no-one mentioned them. It was rather sad.

"Yes. Now where were we? There's been so much going on, these last weeks, I've rather lost the trail," Mr. Rode said.

Here Toby could have said, "Oh yes, The Island. How's it going, sir?" But my Toby was too clever for that. It was his job to remember just where the ancestor-hunt had got to, not to ask questions about The Place of Many Palms.

"William Rode. Younger son of the Mrs. Rode who lived in Water Lane, Ware. He set up a bicycle-repair shop near St. Albans."

"Ah yes. I remember now. To St. Albans, then."

Heaven knows I will not bore you for the thousandth time telling how we got there, as I am sure all you care about now is The Island and so did we.

When we got to Saint Albans the part we entered by was rather pretty. Old, with square creamy houses and lots of greenery. Toby suggested we should go to the nearest large garage and enquire if they knew of a William Rode who repaired bicycles.

"It could still be bicycles, you see, if the place exists at all, as there's been such a revival in bicycling these last few years. Students, and older housewives, use them a lot, especially in a country town," he explained.

You know, we were lucky in all that ancestor-hunting caper. Because, at the first garage we asked, though everyone was tremendously busy, and the harrassed men in white overalls looked sullen when they found Mr. Rode didn't want the car taken to pieces and put together again (taking six weeks), a voice piped up just as we were turning baffled away——

"There's that new gerridge, Jim, down Lacey way."

This came from an old man who was dabbing at something with an oily rag in a corner and keeping well out of the way.

He didn't wear overalls, and I thought perhaps he hung round, opening doors, or telling people they were all right on the left when they were driving out of the garage, and so forth.

"George here knows all about it, seemingly. He'll tell you," said the man we'd been talking to, walking away. I expect they weren't so bad to George in that garage as you might expect. Mr. Rode was plainly American, a tip was certain, and this man had left the way open for George to get it.

But he wouldn't come out of his corner. Stayed there, squatting down beside an inactive-looking car and rubbing part of the right back wheel. We had to go over and speak to him. He peered up at us from under an ancient cap.

"That's the only name of Rode I know hereabout, and I've lived here from a boy. Eighty next birthday."

"A great age," said Toby, bored, but, as always, on duty.

"Yes, that's right. Tisn't exactly the same name, as you might say, but comes near to it. I remember it because there's this gerridge and snackbar just opened there. They had someone off the telly down to do it. Crowds there was, and photos in the paper and all—Roadknight's Corner, it's called."

"And where is it, did you say?"

"Just outside Lacey, on the Watford Road about three miles on the north side. Starting building round there. I

remember when it was fields up to the edge of the town . . .
Thank you, thank you very much indeed, sir."

It must have been a big tip because his face absolutely lit
up. Perhaps it was a pound. Old people simply can't take in,
Toby says, that a pound is now only worth sevenpence or
whatever it is worth. (Or am I thinking of Income Tax? But
never mind.)

"That's our highwayman," said Mr. Rode, when we were
in the car again. "Now Toby—to the Watford Road!"

"I feel as if the Bow Street Runners were after us," said
Mrs. R., laughing and pushing the corny hat a bit further off
her head.

I often think it must be nice to be elderly and frivolous.
Such small things seem to excite them.

Oh good heavens, I now find that I have missed out a fairly
important part of the story.

About two weeks after Guy's death, when Toby was beginning to worry about whether the Rodes had dropped us, he
had told them about Jabez Roadknight, one day over the
telephone.

Explaining that he had kept it dark up until then because
they might feel insulted.

But no, they were amused and interested, and had it not
been for their being very occupied with business about The
Island they would have begun at once to follow up the clue.

Imagine my forgetting that. It was all the grief and excitement to do with Guy's death that drove it out of my mind.

All the way there we discussed the new development,
wondering whether this William Rode had had a place where
the garage was now, or whether they'd seen the name somewhere and taken it because they liked it, and so forth. I was
longing to get round to The Island but the circumstances
simply prevented it.

When we got to Roadknight's Corner, it was a crossroads.

Or rather, three roads, because the ones to London, Watford and little invisible Lacey, which was two and a half miles away down in a dip, met here. It was a good position for a garage, because the roads crossed on a small hill. You could see for quite a long way around.

There was a new garage with petrol pumps and the usual accessories and, beside it, a long, low snack bar with a smallish but extra-modern house at one side. It was all noticeably smart, not tatty at all, tidy and fresh. And over the snack-bar's door and its long clean glass windows hung a painted sign—a highwayman in ruffles and cocked hat, holding a pistol, and showing white teeth in laughter beneath his mask. And painted under it in crimson the words—"Roadknight's Corner".

"All very prosperous and healthy," said Mr. Rode, peering about, "Well, well, well. Someone here is on the up and up, I guess."

"Good-morning. Your money or your life—or perhaps the lady would honour me by dancing a minuet?" said a voice behind us, and we all turned and there was a large man dressed as if he were going fishing, in a thick jersey and rough trousers tucked into knee-high boots.

"Are you the owner of this very attractive-looking . . . joint?" asked Mr. Rode.

"I am. John Fletcher is my name. From the States, of course. Welcome," and he bowed, pretending to sweep off an imaginary hat.

We were getting out of the car, as I think we all felt this was going to be a lengthy business. Toby, I knew, was disliking Mr. Fletcher at sight—his fishing clothes and his way of talking.

"We are doing the characteristic American thing, looking up my ancestors," said Mr. Rode, "and our researches have

188

led us to Roadknight's Corner. I see that you have restored what must have been the original spelling."

"Boiling gravy—are you descended from old Jabez?" cried Mr. Fletcher, practically seizing us, "why, I shouldn't be here, none of us would, Liz my wife, and the brats, and me, if it weren't for him. Come in, come in, and let the heavy drinking begin. I'll tell you all about it."

He whisked us into a small opening off the elegant snack bar, which was surprisingly untidy and even slightly cosy, and shoo'ed off a dirty little girl who was lying on a sofa reading an Enid Blyton book ("the only reader in the family. A throw-back," he explained, as she trailed out through the door still reading). "Sit down, sit down. What do you take?"

The cupboard he flung open was crammed with every possible drink, from vodka to stone ginger beer. I saw both.

When we all had our drinks he sat down on the sagging ancient sofa, looking huge, and smiled on us.

There was something nice about him, and I think it was prosperity. The place was plainly doing very well, and he did not have to *pretend* to be hearty and cheerful. He could be his natural self.

"You don't want the story of my life—four kids and a fifth on the way and still in love—" he said, "I'll tell you about this place. Good enough?"

"Unless you have the urge to communicate," said Mr. Rode, and Mr. Fletcher roared. He seemed easily amused, and he reminded me, being so large and loud, of Mrs. Raven. Perhaps that was the cause of Toby's dislike.

"When we came here, two years ago," he began, "there was nothing but a derelict cottage and a filthy little café, both boarded up. It had been a stamping ground for all the local teds and tarts until the couple who ran it—Hudson by name and nothing to do with the Roadknights—just walked out one day and left it. Money owing everywhere. They tried to disappear but I found them, and bought the café and six acres."

He stopped, and drank some beer.

"They got a fair-ish price. Not what it was worth. But it was all I had and they were glad to get it. I'd always had my eye on this place since I staggered back from the battlefields (six years in the Navy). I'm a Hertfordshire man, I was born down there, in Lacey-in-the-dip, and as a boy I remember old Mr. and Mrs. Roadknight, who served teas in their garden over the week-ends. Traffic wasn't such a headache in those days, of course. It was a nice little place. I remember the red apples on their trees. I was on the road, pushing a new aperitif, for years after the war, and couldn't raise the capital. But a friend lent me some, at last, and it came just in time to make the offer for this place. Bingo."

He drank more beer. I could almost see the question forming on Toby's lips: if you are a Hertfordshire man, born in Lacey-in-the-dip, why dress as if going tuna-fishing? The sea is a hundred miles away. He was lounging back in his chair, looking faintly amused.

But I liked John Fletcher. He was cheerful, and at least he was *working*. I wouldn't have said this to my Toby, and I felt disloyal even to have the thought. All the same, I had it.

"Old Mr. Roadknight used to say his father and his grandfather had lived in the cottage before him. The old boy, the grandfather, had a little shed at the back where he mended punctures and kept the odd spare tyre for cyclists, and later on in the early nineteen hundreds he began to do the same for motorists. (You know how those early models were always breaking down.) He used to say the family was descended from one Jabez Roadknight, a highwayman. (Road-knight, Knight of the Road. Nice example of folk-irony, isn't it? I was pleased, I can tell you, when I found that. Local history's been my hobby since I was fifteen. *God*

190

*gave man all earth to love, But, since our hearts are small
. . .* do you admire Kipling? Great man. Bloody fools don't
like his politics . . . as if Imperialism wasn't a perennial. But
it'll all come back, you'll see. Where was I? Oh yes—.)
Apparently the family name was originally R-O-A-D——"

"I am Clay R-O-D-E," said Mr. Rode, smiling.

"Are you, though! You must come from the grandfather's
younger brother—he went to the States in one of those big
waves of emigrants in the '80's."

"That's him, my grandfather," Mr. Rode nodded, and I
glanced at Toby, remembering that sentence in dead old Mr.
Cranford's note—*'the eldest boy went completely to the bad,
went to London and incurred a series of sentences for petty
theft. There is no trace of what became of him.'*

Not completely to the bad. Our Mr. Rode's grandfather.

"Did well for himself, eh?" laughed John Fletcher.

"Not too badly," said Mr. Rode, with what I suppose is
called a *poker face,* or *deadpan.* But I would say *demurely*
was a truer word. There was just a glint. And, you know, he
is more like a moose (that Canadian animal with all those
horns) than a horse, really. It is not a gentle or a weak face.
A moose can charge at you.

"I'm glad to hear it. Always pleased to hear of someone
doing well," Mr. Fletcher said heartily and then Mrs. Rode
said, in her pretty voice:

"So am I, Mr. Fletcher. And I guess you are, here?"

"Doing well? Boiling gravy, m'dear lady, the place is a—
a—gold mine. A ber-linking gold-mine. Especially at week-
ends, when we get all the Sat. and Sun. motorists from
Watford and St. Albans and people driving up to town for a
show from further out."

"And where do all the local teds and tarts go now?" Toby
asked languidly. Mr. Fletcher sent him a straight look. I

could see that he could tell when someone was trying to take the micky out from him.

"I don't know. Or care." He got up from the sofa. "Well, now, it's after twelve. I won't ask you to lunch in the house because all the children are at home thanks to a measles epidemic at their school, God aid us, and I *hope* you don't know what *that's* like. But the snackery will do its damnedest for you. Come along!"

I *wished* Toby would like ordinary cheerful people. He is always saying, *why is his life so difficult?* Well, I'm sure that if he would only enjoy people more, it wouldn't be. He is only interested in characters like his elderly Lady Vanessa. And what had he got out of her? So far as I knew, just nothing, except possibly a bad dinner in some decaying ancestral mansion.

I only saw Mr. Fletcher lose his cheerful air once during our whole visit, and that was just as we were sitting down in the pretty, warm, elegant snack bar. "I say, if you *were* thinking of making an offer for the place, will you write me?" he said to Mr. Rode in a hurried murmur. "I wouldn't want Liz, my wife, to know. You see, I'd never sell. It's the darlin' of me heart, Roadknight's Corner."

Then, oh *then*, I heard Mr. Rode murmur that he had no such idea, indeed, they'd just bought an island—mutter, murmur, couldn't hear any more—and were thinking of— fade out.

Oh, tantalizing. And what about the Lelands?

As you may imagine, all through our good, hot, snack lunch I was longing to retail this piece of conversation to Toby. But what with the noise, and the drinking, and the conversation, and all the measle-threatened children coming to peer at us round the door and being scooped back by Liz-my-wife (fair hair in a ponytail, gingham muu-muu, cross

192

expression) and so forth, there was no peace and quiet for a moment.

But I did get a good look at the menu out of the corner of my eye, and thought, no wonder Roadknight's Corner was a gold-mine. Boiling gravy, it was pricey. No competition for miles, you see, and everything so attractive and gay.

I didn't wonder that dashing Jabez Roadknight on the sign outside was laughing under his mask. His Corner might have taken to earning an honest living in its old age, but certainly it was keeping up the family tradition of highway robbery.

XXII

WELL, after this everything seemed to happen at once. You know how it sometimes is.

The ancestor-hunt was finished. We had come to the end of the trail. Mr. Fletcher told us, as we sat over coffee and brandy with him and Liz-my-wife, that the Roadknights of the Corner had been childless. The old man had always said that any kinsfolk they had must be over in America—as, indeed, they were.

"So I guess if we meant to hunt up any more we'll have to start in Maine," Mr. Rode said in a thoughtful voice, drinking up his brandy.

"But what about your island? Sun, blue sea, gorgeous Hawaian belles?" said Mr. Fletcher—not seriously, I could see.

"Ah yes. The Island," Mr. Rode answered still in a musing voice, and looked at his brandy glass. Liz-my-wife spoke to me for the first time.

"You going too?" she asked abruptly. Now wasn't that a wizard chance to exclaim 'Oh, I don't know. That depends,' or something of that kind?

But Mr. Rode didn't look up, and neither he nor Mrs. Rode said a word, and of course at that moment a child fell down and broke its leg or something, and began shrieking, and a foreign girl came charging in, carrying it, with another hanging round her legs and also bellowing, and what with her jabbering, and Liz-my-wife jerking the children out of the room with a cross good-bye at us, any chance we had of seeing where we stood was completely lost.

Mr. Rode began to get up.

"Well——" he said.

And in a few minutes we had finished saying our hearty good-byes, and had got ourselves into the car and were driving away.

Mrs. Rode, who was sitting at the back with me, turned round as she finished waving to the Fletchers. Mr., and Liz-my-wife, and the foreign girl and all the measley children were congregated outside the snack house and all madly waving.

"Meetings and partings," said Mrs. Rode, with a kind of sigh. "How very lovely the countryside looks to-day, Nancy."

Meetings and partings! I ask you. How I wished I could say, "Mrs. Rode, do tell me about The Island."

But it was no use. For some reason, I could not. I think it was because they had made it plain that they didn't want us asking questions. Tactfully. Not unkindly. But quite, quite plain.

"Yes. Kind of rich," I said.

"It's been such fun," she went on, in her little sub-deb voice, "working out this crazy notion of Clay's. He's the one who has the crazy notions, you know. I'm the sane one." She glanced at me. "I expect it's like that with you and Toby."

"It is rather," I said, not giving anything away.

"What are your plans for the fall?" she said next, after a little silence, and then I did begin to feel excited, because in the next few moments I might hear what was going to happen to us.

"We haven't any," I said in a gay carefree voice, "we shall just wait and see what comes up."

She looked at me again, and I thought that she was going to say something. But she didn't. She only slipped her arm through mine, and turned away to look at the view.

I was so disappointed. Not a word. Oh, why did Toby and

195

I have to be in this position, when we couldn't ask the plain question—*What are you going to do about us? Take us with you?*

"We must have a really gorgeous time to-night," she said presently, "as it's—Clay," leaning forward, "did you get the tickets?"

As it's the last time, I wondered?

But there were no more hints that we could work on that day. Everything went on just as usual. We talked about Roadknight's Corner and the Fletchers, and Mr. Rode said more than once how satisfactory it was to have hunted his English ancestors down right to the extinction of the branch, and added that he had certainly seen something of the real England, thanks to Toby. I was pleased at this, for my Toby. And Mr. Rode said it was "a permanent addition to his store of world-knowledge", this knowing bits of gloomy old Herts. quite well.

I do think older people are *inexplicable*.

Although everything went on as usual, I had a kind of final feeling. Not a word was said, but I had it, and I know that Toby had it too. It was suspicious in itself, this not saying one word about future plans for any of us, now that the ancestor-hunting was finished. Though we had never become really intimate with them, the Rodes knew us well enough to make it natural to say *something* about what would happen next.

But they didn't. Not one word.

We parted after a gorgeous lunch, and it was arranged that we should all meet to go to *Vanity Fair* that evening. Which we did. Dreamy. And to supper afterwards. And they said goodnight to us, it seemed to me, more than usually kindly, leaning out of their taxi window and beaming. Mrs. R. kissed me.

196

"Good-bye," said Toby again, and as they drove away he added "for ever."

He stood there, hatless, in his dark evening coat, in the soft red glare of the crowded street, staring after them.

"What do you mean?" All round us, the homeward-going crowd was surging, laughing, chattering about the show.

"You'll see," he said in a grim voice. "We're dropped."

"Oh don't be so dreary," I said, as we got into a cab, not having hired the car that evening.

"I know I'm right. Shut up about it now. Oh, why is my life so difficult? Just kiss me— —"

So all the way home we kissed.

That night was so happy. But the next morning, when he telephoned the Chandos about twelve to suggest that we should meet for drinks, we were told they had gone.

...Gone. That morning. About ten o'clock. No address left for forwarding letters, no message for a Mr. Leland, nothing. Vanished into space, and our hopes of The Island with them.

Toby put down the receiver, and stood looking at me.

"We've had it. I'm sorry, Idle," he said.

"Don't mind about it, darling," I said, "something's sure to turn up. How much money have we got?"

"Seventeen pounds. Their next cheque is due on Friday, and I'm pretty sure we can count on it coming."

"There may be a letter."

"There'll be a note from him, thanking me for arranging it all. Nothing else."

"I *wish* you wouldn't be so dreary."

"How can I help it? It's bad enough for me, but I feel I've landed you in all this, too."

"Oh, Toby *do not be so*—unrealistic. We're young, we're in good health, we've got each other. We aren't even in debt. It isn't so frightful. We've got this flat. So do cheer up."

"I will *not* take a regular job. I will NOT," said my husband, beginning to work himself up, "crawling out of bed when the alarm goes, three hours with dreary morons killing time, filthy lunch in a smelly café, more killing time with morons— —"

"No-one is asking you to," I said. "Let's go to the cinema."

So we went. I suppose because he was in a depressed mood, Toby insisted on a film with someone called Inger Bergmann mixed up somehow in it and I agreed because I thought it was Ingrid Bergmann, and then it was so *dreary*. Symbolic.

We came away annoyed and kind of flattened, and then when we got back to the flat things suddenly became much worse.

There was a letter, for Toby, and he simply tore it open.

I was watching him ,and I saw his face go pale with anger and dismay.

He swore, and threw the letter down.

"Bad news?" I said. Any news from now on, I was beginning to feel, is bound to be. (And that, as you may know, is not like me.)

"No—yes, well, yes, it is. You may as well know, you'll have to some time. It's from my mother. She wants money."

I didn't say, "Oh, I thought she was dead." After all, he hadn't even said she was. He had only let me think it.

"How much?" I asked.

"Ten pounds. She's got herself behindhand over payments for some patent bed or other, because she bought some clothes —I don't know. Anyway, she's behind with the instalments and they've sent her a solicitor's letter. I thought you could get away with that kind of thing nowadays."

I sat there, thinking. Of course she would have to have ten pounds. It would leave us with only seven. But I could be a waitress or baby-sit or something, couldn't I?

I was not going to be got down.

198

Toby was sitting opposite, leaning forward in his chair, and I could tell by his expression that he wanted to talk.

"How much did Guy tell you?" he began. "Do you know about old St. Merryn?"

I nodded.

"Oh, you do. Well, I admit it looks black. I don't know how Guy put it to you—I don't expect his version was very highly-coloured, because he was a gentleman and my friend," (my poor Toby). "I still don't know why he had to tell you at all, but on the whole I'm glad he did. I used to send my mother money every month out of what the old boy let me have. Then we had a row—he's as *jealous* as a queer, I'll admit that, but so are some parents—and when I renounced the allowance, I gave up sending. That's how she's got into this jam, I expect."

"You had better——" I began, when Toby flung out his hand.

"Stop it, Nancy. I won't stand for it."

I stared. "Stand for what?"

"Being bossed. It's the last straw."

"I was only going to say——"

"I'm sure you were, that's just it. *I'll* make the decisions, thank you. I've been through enough, these last three months, wondering, trying to think things out, and then Guy getting killed—and worrying because I married you——"

"Toby!"

"Don't be a half-wit, you know what I mean. I mean, we've nothing at the back of us and I'm responsible for you—and the Rodes dropping us, and now this——" he picked up the letter.

You know, sometimes you would think it was Toby who had the Continental ancestors, not me. I think it's my mother in me, that keeps me calm. She was very placid. Toby does get so worked up.

199

"I'm sorry," I said, not too meekly, "but let's try to look at it as it *is*. *Here* we are, seventeen— —"

"Nearly eighteen," Toby groaned.

"Nearly eighteen, and nearly twenty-seven. Strong, healthy. Sitting in a warm comfortable rent-free flat. Our lives before us— —"

"And seven pounds in cash."

"You're going to send it, then?" I said, breaking off my lecture, which I could see was not going to have any effect.

"Of course I'm going to send it." He stared gloomily at the floor.

It now occurred to me that he might write for help to Mr. St. M. But I didn't say anything which might suggest it. I wanted to be rid of that old man. I didn't believe there was so much harm in it as poor Guy had hinted, but I still thought Toby would be better standing on his own two feet.

Or what about Randy, and all those other wild and well-bred young men he used to keep in touch with and be so careful never to borrow from?

But I didn't mention them, either. He would think of them, no doubt, soon enough. And I still thought he must begin to rely on himself.

"You must have been in bad spots before," I said, "haven't you, honeybug?"

"Yes, worse. But then I hadn't got you. God, Nancy, can't you see that that's what's getting under my skin? I'm worried for you."

I got up and went across to him and hugged him. He seemed glad to hold me.

"Well don't be. We shall manage. And now—I don't mean to make the decisions, truly—but that money had better go off to your mother."

"Would you like to come down to Colchester and meet her?" asked Toby, suddenly, looking down into my face.

"It might be a good idea," I replied, with cautiousness.

In truth I didn't want to go down to Colchester and meet her at all. Remembering that Guy had said she lived in a bed-sitter and was as good as dead.

I really had had enough of oldies, though thank heaven the ones living round us were now all provided for and as gay as possible—tea-parties and tottering up and down the stairs in and out of each other's flats and taking six hours to choose a wallpaper. But enough.

And then of course Mrs. Leland turned out to be absolutely different from what I had expected and not as good as dead at all.

She had short black hair and a loudish voice and seemed rather frighteningly set on staying alive as long as possible without much money to do it on. She was an intense sort of woman, whose brownish eyes bored through you, and her bed-sitter was all done on that G-plan and had indoor plants and a room divider and a lot of that red wood modern decorators use, shiny and immaculate. She struck me as making the very utmost of what little she had.

I didn't like her.

I know people are always supposed not to like their mothers-in-law. There are all those jokes, and I must confess that I wasn't prepared to like Mrs. Leland, because I wanted Toby all to myself.

But she seemed a hollow kind of woman. I don't expect it was her fault (actually, I preferred Mrs. Rawlings, Rays and all).

Thank goodness, Mrs. L. didn't make the slightest scene or fuss about anything. She rattled away about shows and books and films; she seemed to *belong* to a lot of things in Colchester, like dramatic societies and bridge clubs and even political associations (she kept on saying that *she* had *always* been a Liberal).

Though her eyes did bore into me, I don't think I really interested her, and I was glad.

Oh, yes, she also had this part-time job in a pet shop, that poor Guy had mentioned. We saw the shop out of our taxi window on the way to the station and it was rather a grand shop, no smelly monkeys or anything, but expensive dogs, and offering to strip them and so forth. So it can't have been a 'rotten little job', though this being with animals rather wrote her off, with me. So unhealthy.

So I did think she was all right, and when in the train Toby casually suggested we should drop her, I agreed.

We had enough to occupy our minds and time, and if we did not have to worry about Mrs. Leland, that was all right.

But I did tell Toby that he must go on sending her money, as soon as he had any. The G-plan furniture, and her social life, and being a Liberal, was all she had, and I did think it would be hard if she had to give any of it up for lack of money.

And then would you *imagine*, a few days later when we were in an even worse state because of something else that happened about which I will tell you in a moment, an *awful* letter came from her, saying she was so lonely she wished she could *die* and what *use* was she and her only son *despised* her and she could see he had married a girl who would *despise her too*. And she was his *useless*, *worn out* old mother.

"Old Atkins must have let her down," said Toby, after reading this somewhat shattering letter.

"Who's old Atkins?" (Not that I cared. This transformation of Toby's mother did seem the final straw.)

I was sitting on the sofa (drinking some gin given to me by Mrs. Rawlings, who had been drifting about for days like some dizzy Father Christmas, suddenly popping bottles of scent and half-pints of champagne into the arms of anyone who happened to be around).

"He runs the shop she works in. She was hoping he'd marry her. He lost his wife last year."

"For love, or money?" I asked. (All this was news to me.)

Toby glanced at me.

"Oh, not only for money. I think she really is lonely. She's quite brave, my mother, you know."

Wishing she didn't have to be, I drank some more gin.

We were far too busy wondering where we'd sleep that night to give much thought to Toby's mother's shattered hopes.

I will tell you about that.

Only first let us *finish*, for goodness sake, with Mrs. Hannah (I ask you. The ultimate and final straw. *Hannah*) Leland.

You will not be surprised to hear that early next morning we had a 'phone call from Colchester and there was Hannah, choking with excitement and relief and going to marry Atkins after all.

Sometimes I wish everyone over thirty would die quietly in the night.

"You're not at all like her, are you?" I said idly, glad to stop discussing the situation about which I'm going to tell you.

"Not in the least. I'm like my father. He was a—a quieter type. I think she more or less wore him out, worrying him to make more money, and think she feels guilty about it, you know, and always will. That's why she rushes about, and talks so much."

I was a bit low, that morning, and it did just occur to me to ask him if he thought there was *one single person*, in the *whole world*, who was happy, and didn't have a secret sorrow?

But I refrained. What good would it do?

Anyway, thank God, it was fade out, with wedding bells, for Hannah. And so (as my mother's ancient books used to say) she passes from my tale.

I will now tell you about the next disturbing happening.

XXIII

I SHALL have to go back a little way.

On the evening of the day we got Mrs. Leland's letter, the second, despairing one, we were sitting over a drink, wondering whether to go out for supper or eat tomatoes and eggs in the flat, and I had left the living-room door open to catch the breeze, because it had been a stifling day.

I was persuading Toby not to ask Mrs. Rawlings for a loan.

"It wouldn't be for more than fifty pounds," he was saying. (Thank What, or Whoever, it was that sometimes saved us from disaster, he was wearing one of his own shirts.)

And then, we heard the front door open. We heard the key turn in the lock and then we heard it shut, quite loudly. We stared at each other, with open mouths, and Toby swung his legs down from the arm of his chair and I sat upright. Still staring, at the open door of the living-room now, we heard sounds of someone coming towards us.

The next instant a man walked into the room, a stranger. He was dark and sturdy, wearing a good American suit, and hatless, and he looked like a friend of Guy's or Randy's— prosperous, and well-connected.

He nodded, and said, "Oh . . . good-evening. You're Murray's friends, I suppose. I'm afraid I'll have to ask you to get out at once. I want the place."

He went straight over to the telephone, and I remember thinking *that's cool*, and then realizing who he was. The man from Oriel, the real tenant of this place. The man supposedly dead in Algeria or somewhere. Whose shirts Toby had been wearing.

"Sorry," he said, over his shoulder, and seemed to forget us. He stood, with bent head and the receiver to his ear, waiting.

Toby mouthed at me to go into the next room, and I was so dazed that I went.

I expected him to follow. But he didn't, and soon I heard them talking, though I couldn't hear what was said. I fiddled about aimlessly for some time, wondering what was going to happen to us now, and at last I became cheesed off with being thrust aside like a gangster's moll, as they were called in the ancient films, and combed my hair and did my face and went back into the living-room.

"Oh, hullo, darling," said Toby, who was looking furious, "it's all right. We can stay here to-night. At three pounds ten a head," he said viciously, glaring at Oriel-man.

Oriel-man was looking faintly amused.

"I really am sorry——" he said, "but for private reasons I can't get to the bank, and until Wednesday I've no money. You've had three months here rent free. You mustn't get ideas, you know," he ended gently.

He spoke to us as if we'd been two children who'd got in the way while he was robbing a bank. (As perhaps he was.) I wish I could make you feel how frightening he was. Guy and Randy and Toby weren't knights in shining armour but at least they seemed human. This man made you feel that if you got in his way he would hurt you badly. I had never seen anyone like him, until now.

We got out of the flat as quickly as possible. I dug up a ten-bob note from somewhere and we dined at a greasy little place on the edge of Hampstead, almost in silence, we were so depressed. It didn't seem worth while talking.

When we got back, the man wasn't there. A bed had been made up on the divan, with some silk pyjamas lying on it, and I averted my eyes from them and sank into a chair, thankful to have him gone, while Toby shut the windows and drew the curtains against the lowering summer evening.

"He's dangerous all right," he said dejectedly at last, as he came and sat down opposite me, "speak no ill of the dead —but what was old Guy doing, tangling with a character like that?"

You know, I believe in the depths of his mind Toby's heroes were Robin Hood and Raffles, that character who played cricket and was secretly a thief. (My father used to say Raffles was a *minor myth*, and threw light on the English character.) Toby wanted big money but he also wanted to remain a decent Public School man. I suppose it could be done. Oriel-man still had the voice and the manner—but, boiling gravy! he smelt of badness.

"Let's go to bed," I said, getting up wearily, "we may as well get our money's worth. It's half-past nine."

"My God, is that all? I thought it was three in the morning."

"He has made up a bed on the divan," I pointed out, "he might have turned us out of the bedroom."

"So I should ruddy well hope, at three ten a head, the swine. He just asked me how much I had and took it off me. What one would call moral force, I suppose . . . You get undressed, if you like. I'm going to do some work." He had got his address book, and was turning the pages.

Poor Toby. For the next hour he really *abased* himself, grimly ringing up acquaintance after acquaintance, using up all the names and numbers carefully hoarded in that little book for years, since he and Guy were at school together. They were all West End numbers, and sometimes servants answered—I heard them—and Toby had to wait while they went to give the message. And not one single result. Not an invitation to stay, or a loan, or offer of a desirable job—

nothing. Only excuses, and half-promises, and people being away or out.

It did hurt me. I *felt* so, for my Toby, driven to crawling.

At last, pale and defeated, he hung up the receiver and looked at me.

"No use. We've had it. I'm sorry, I really and truly am, Nancy. To-morrow, I'll get a job."

I went to him and put my arms round him.

"Poor love," I said.

He held me close. "It's been a long dream," he said, "and I—oh, I don't know. In a way I've enjoyed it and then sometimes it would hurt like mad. I wish I'd never . . ."

"Never married me?" I whispered.

"No, oh no. Never that. Only, I could play about by myself, you see, and now I can't because I must look after you. No—I was only going to say, sometimes I wish I'd never started pretending. But never mind now. For God's sake, let's get some sleep."

He did. But for some time I lay awake. Because I was wondering what job he could get. Only a day or two ago I had been chatting with a greengrocer who told me that a man offering to work delivering vegetables and so forth had asked twenty pounds a week. Such jobs were to be had.

But . . . Toby delivering vegetables?

Never mind. I could get one. Women don't have to keep up their dignity.

In the small hours, that terrifying Oriel-man came back—*with someone else*. We heard their voices growling away. Of course, he had a right to bring strangers in, as it was his flat, but we had got used to thinking of it as *ours*.

At last we heard the front door shut, and Oriel-man moving about from room to room and then lights being switched off, and silence.

It was strange to think of that creature lying down to sleep, settling his head into the pillow like everyone else. But of course, even beasts of prey go to sleep.

In thrillers, the gay young married pair score off the master criminal with no trouble at all. But in real life criminals are not like they are in thrillers, and we did not know even how to begin scoring.

But morning came, in its usual way in August, and there was the sun shining into our room. I was just yawning and stretching when the 'phone rang, and I heard O.-M. talking to someone. As Toby sat up, the door opened and round it came the dark face unsmiling.

"For you," he said, to Toby, "you'll be out by ten, won't you." He shut the door, and as we got out of bed, still half-awake, we heard him leave the flat.

That 'phone call brings us to where we were some pages back, because it was Toby's mum announcing her glad betrothal to Atkins.

Oriel-man had eaten all our eggs for his breakfast. I was furious but Toby, who I think has a softer nature than mine, said it made him seem more human.

"What I mind most of all"—Toby was saying, finishing his first cigarette of the day while I sat on the sofa, as previously told, and swigged gin, "what I really mind is the way he seems to have sized us up and decided we don't count. He doesn't even bother to take precautions about us. We might go to the police."

"How could we, Toby? We haven't any evidence."

"Evidence or not, I'm sure he's up to something very nasty indeed."

"Oh well never mind him now. It's nine. We must be out of here in one hour. Where to?"

"God alone knows," Toby said, then he exclaimed—"Your Aunt Edie! We'll try her."

"Oh Toby, don't be silly. She only has her pension, and

that commission she makes on selling the mail order goods, and her knitting money. And her cottage has only two rooms and one outside loo. You could never bear it."

"Hasn't she any savings?" Toby muttered, not looking at me, and then, at that very moment, which I honestly think was the lowest to which we two ever sank, there came a knock at the front door.

I ran to open it—being always of a hopeful nature—and there stood Mrs. Rawlings.

Wearing a new purple dressing-gown that the designer intended to look majestic, and her head done up in a Liberty scarf. Looking anxious.

"Dear child, I am so relieved to see you apparently safe and sound," she began at once, "though sorry that you should feel compelled to drink gin at nine in the morning. Is that a sign of evil forces all around you? I fear it must be, because ever since seven o'clock last night I have been aware of the most dreadful vibrations I have ever encountered, in the whole extent of my researches into the Occult, emanating from your flat. At first——"

"Oh do come in. I *am* so glad to see you," I said, almost hugging her. I had a feeling that now things would turn for the better.

"Well, I will, dear child." She stepped, as though into a drain or sewer or something, over our threshold. "Emanations of this dreadful strength and nature must not be avoided, but *encountered* and *resisted*. At first I thought they might be lingering on in the building, generated by an unpleasant, though finally satisfactory, interview which Mr. Hayes and I had yesterday with one of the greedy and unfortunate creatures who own the flats. (That is, they now own them no longer.) But then I thought, no. Stupid, avaricious, blind as they are, they could not send forth vibrations of such power."

I knew Toby would be groaning in his heart at having to

talk about vibrations and rays at this moment. But for once I could not help his troubles. I led Mrs. Rawlings into the living-room. He gave her a sickly smile

"Terrible," she said, looking around her and shuddering.

Toby looked faintly surprised.

"I can't feel them as you do, Mrs. Rawlings," I said quickly, having had a smashing idea, "but there is a dreadful man staying here—come back to live, I mean. He's the tenant. (We were only lent it, you know.) He came back last night."

Mrs. Rawlings looked at me thoughtfully.

"He's *your* tenant now," I went on. "I was just wondering —could you possibly ask him to let us stay on for a few days? Just until we find somewhere else?"

Toby was now sitting up and looking hopeful.

But Mrs. R. shook her head. "I cannot face him, dear child," she said. "I have not the necessary spiritual force. It would need a White Adept."

I think that's what she said. She spoke seriously, without her usual smiling wanderiness.

"I should only be overcome, and things would be worse for you than ever. You see, nothing is so simple as you think. It is not even *what* you think— —"

Here Toby cut in, slightly impatiently.

"Can't you just say you'll throw him out if he doesn't let us stay here?"

"No, I cannot," Mrs. Rawlings said with dignity. "I have just told you that I have not the spiritual force to encounter and defeat this man. I shall have to take time, and get in harmony with the Rays— —"

Here they were. And useless, as usual. She had said herself that they hadn't even helped her with her Pools win.

"I *shall* dispose of him," she ended calmly, "so far as this flat and myself are concerned. Though not, I fear, finally. That must be left to Other Influences. But what I can do is to

invite you both, most warmly, to stay with me until . . .
something turns up." She smiled.

"Oh, you *are* an *angel*!" I cried, "and we can help you with
the books!"

The next moment we were bounding round the flat, fling-
ing our things into our cases in a way which ordinarily Toby
would have scorned while Mrs. R. tottered downstairs to
open a bottle of champagne.

All that day, the sun shone. We got to work on the books,
which Mrs. Rawlings was moving for the first time in about
thirty years to have the flat redecorated, and stood on the top
of shaking ladders, and were bathed in clouds of dust. I liked
it.

We were helping Mrs. R., and it was a cheerful atmosphere,
and better than sitting in some café wondering what on earth
we were going to do and spinning out our last two shillings.

I don't think Toby liked it as much as I did, but he did pull
himself together, and he worked hard.

Mrs. R. drifted about, frying mushrooms, and smiling at us.
The Rays, I suppose, looked on approvingly.

And by the very afternoon post came a letter from Randy
Brookes for Toby, apologizing for the delay and paying ten
guineas to us for that day we had posed for the photographs
outside the pub. So we were safe financially for at least a
week.

That night, after a gorgeous supper with wine, we slept in
an ancient double bed, with soft, worn, sheets, surrounded by
dusty books and vases of flowers, while Mrs. R. turned in on a
kind of nun's pallet in the living-room. It was as cosy and
peaceful as you can imagine.

We did hear O.-M. creaking stealthily about overhead but
we shut our minds to him.

I am now coming to the part where something apparently
too good to be true happens.

We waylaid the postman every day, as we thought it quite likely that O.-M., though scorning us, might steal our letters in hope of cash. And when we had been with Mrs. R. for three days, and there had been no sounds overhead of O.-M. for twenty-four hours, and we were beginning to wonder if he had finally cleared out, *a letter came from the Rodes.*

By air mail, and Express, and so forth. With two air tickets. For us, for Toby and me. To take us to Marseilles, in France.

I do not underline the above sentence, leaving it, after all our ups and downs, to impress you.

Imagine to yourself. We were to join them on The Island, the warm, lazy, blue-circled, scented, Place of Many Palms.

For hours, I couldn't believe it. I sat in Mrs. R.'s flat, among the piles of books and the flowers and dust, staring at the tickets, reading and re-reading the affectionate note accompanying them—"looking forward to seeing you both for a good long visit."

And I could not believe that our dream had come true.

Toby was wild with excitement, and very cocky because this was what he had planned for, and always hoped— though not always trusted—would happen. He could not settle, but drifted from flat to flat, kissing the female oldies who had tottered in to resume their joyful game of choosing wallpapers (some of them had been at it for a week) and who stayed to marvel and congratulate, and admire. He disappeared in a taxi immediately after lunch, and came back with a small but perfect wardrobe of tropical clothes, obtained on the never-never, on the strength of his future job as Mr. Rode's social secretary.

He offered to fiddle me one, but I said, no, my peach linen suit would do, to begin with. I had blouses, and thin underclothing.

The tickets were for Friday morning, and we spent a madly

rushed week, getting ourselves inoculated for many unpleasant foreign diseases.

The Rodes had insisted, in their note, on this being done,
and I must confess that it slightly shook me. But I remembered the fuss that Americans always do make about matters
of health.

Some of the diseases 'took', and by Thursday evening, when
Mrs. Rawlings, dear old thing, gave a farewell party for us,
we were both feverish.

But that only added to our gaiety. Because we were too air-
borne with excitement to feel ill.

That *was* a party.

Mrs. R. said we could invite anyone we liked, and simply
everybody came, in spite of the short notice—including Aunt
Edie, who was put up on a camp-bed by Miss de Havilland,
and all Mrs. R.'s old friends, and lots of people we knew.
Even the elderly Lady Vanessa turned up, in a poppet of an
old Renault, looking elegant and hard but talking in a way
about Guy that showed she had liked him very much, and was
slightly knocked out by his going. The Fletchers from Roadknight's Corner were there, and Liz-my-wife looked truly
cheerful (I think she loathed the country) and, oh, my dear
Mrs. Raven, the friend of my orphanhood. Randy Brookes
brought two model girls, famous ones, who stood about,
smiling surprisedly out of their huge eyes, like children at the
Zoo, and who absolutely fascinated Mr. Pegram.

Only Guy wasn't there.

He would have enjoyed it so much. All the evening, while
the champagne flowed and the laughter sounded, underneath
my excitement, I was thinking of Guy, and missing him—I,
who used to be jealous of him while he was alive.

I do think life does some strange things to one.

Toby was thinking of Guy, too, I know. More than once
during the evening, when we exchanged glances across the

crowded room and he made the kissing face at me, he looked sad, and it was because he was thinking of his dead friend.

Poor Guy. Dear Guy. The Red Indians used to believe in a place called The Happy Hunting Grounds, where their warriors found game, and sweet water, and plenty of wood for fires, for evermore. I hope that somewhere in those many mansions there is an endless racing track with a perfect surface, and a car with never a flaw that goes like a bird—The Car, perhaps, put together again and made new—and unwearying spirits to re-fuel and service her. And I hope that there Guy can drive. Drive for ever, with eyes half-shut and the faint happy smile he only had when he was driving, on for ever and ever, for eternity, through the gulfs of Space.

But we enjoyed that party—our last party—Toby and I, in spite of our sadness about Guy. It was an extraordinary, mixed, fantastic occasion, not because anyone was trying to be different or daring, but because everyone there was simply being themselves, and everyone was so different from everybody else. Not wild, either, there were too many people of over seventy present for wildness to break out, in spite of the great quantities of drink served by Mr. Fletcher and Randy Brookes, but truly cheerful, and gay.

In the middle of it all, about eleven o'clock, Mrs. Rawlings drew me aside and whispered that the Really Dreadful Vibrations in our former flat had at last faded out.

"Oh, goody for that," I said. Being rather drunk.

"Yes, dear child. They have been steadily diminishing, for the past twenty-four hours, and now I think we may safely assume that their baneful influence is at an end here."

"Only here?" I said, for she still looked grave.

"Oh yes, I fear so. They will have gone to some other place, to wreak harm there. But I have been concentrating the Rays steadily on your flat, ever since the evil vibrations began to decline, and now *they* are in charge."

She nodded and smiled and drifted away, and as it all seemed part of the general unreality of the evening, I lifted my glass and, saying aloud "Cheerio, Rays", I drained it. Aunt Edie chose this moment, of course, to come up and ask me rather sharply if this island was suitable for having a baby on? But I managed to put her off. That was just Aunt Edie.

I can't say that I remember much about the end of the party. It was all one goldeny sheen of champagne. But I clearly remember the next morning, when everybody, even the oldies who had had a very late night and those little hooligans who used to fire peas at the tenants, assembled to see us drive away.

It was a brilliantly sunny day, and the little crowd stood in the entrance to Rowland Mansions, smiling and waving and calling out messages of good-will and affection—Mr. Pegram, and Miss de Havilland, with Snowy, as usual, looking hatingly at everybody from his place in her arms, and Mr. Haynes, Aunt Edie and Plastic Mac and, of course, dear Mrs. Rawlings. There were some painters and workmen, too, who were already busy with restoring and brightening up the old place, on Mrs. R.'s orders, and no doubt The Rays were hovering somewhere round about, shedding good-will on us all.

"Good luck! Good-bye! Good-bye!"

The oldies waved, the grinning workmen looked down from the scaffolding and waved, and the children cheered shrilly. We waved back, and then the taxi drove away, down through the crowded streets of ancient London, away to the blue seas and warm sands. Carrying us off to our Dream Island, The Place of Many Palms.

XXIV

By the time we arrived at Marseilles, I at least was slightly dazed by the *size* of this world over which we had passed so quickly. Mile upon mile of dim green land or snowy mountains, mile upon mile upon mile, thousands of feet below us. Quite soon, I turned my eyes and thoughts away from it and enjoyed our meals, and fellow-travellers, and the inside of the plane.

Of course at the airport we expected to be met, and we were—but only with an envelope, containing more air tickets!

On to *Aden*, a place I had never heard of.

We were beginning to feel slightly uneasy. Toby *did* know about Aden, and he said it was a ghastly hot rock, and only the British Air Force lived there. However, he hoped that it might lead on to some delicious region with date palms, since coral-reefs were apparently out.

I will shorten this part of our story, as you will want to know what happened.

After hours more dazing travelling, we arrived.

About Aden—the only words I can think of is what a German girl I met at a party called a certain type of young man—"zo primitif".

Aden was just that. Lowering mountains apparently made from dust, the most appalling and blinding heat, a pale spiteful sky, and everything bare and military. Highly depressing. We were too cast down to talk, but waited silently at the airport, with our light smart luggage, feeling entirely lost and wondering what was going to happen to us.

Then this Mr. Cheng came up, Chinese, but speaking flawless English, and took us off in a smaller plane, quite safe, apparently, but full of boxes and bundles and so forth and two uneducated Arab-creatures who smelt frightful and never stopped staring. Mr. Cheng, who seemed friendly enough but cagey, said that they had been working on the mainland but were now coming back to our island to live.

Toby and I exchanged looks of dismay.

Were these our laughing brown natives wreathed in flowers? They were wreathed in the filthiest rags you can imagine. By now, our rosy dreams really had faded, and we were beginning to feel seriously alarmed.

We only had about ten pounds, in English money, and the clothes in our suitcases. Suppose the Rodes never turned up at all, and Mr. Cheng just dumped us in some—dump? He appeared to know the Rodes quite well, but who could be certain? And when Toby tried to pump him, he politely avoided giving any hard news.

We went on for what seemed a week and actually was three hours, over miles and miles of excruciatingly boring sea, and then at last the Arabs got over-excited, and began to chatter like monkeys, and point out of the windows. Down below was a small brown patch in the sea with a tiny blob of dark green in the middle.

That was all. No creaming surf, no purple lagoons, no forests, nothing but this dusty patch. Still, I thought, it may be better when we get down—if we do.

"Place of Many Palms," said Mr. Cheng, smiling at us.

I dared not look at Toby.

Down we went. I was too disturbed, and furious with the Rodes, even to feel afraid that Mr. Cheng would miss the patch and drop us in the sea. (As a matter of fact, he is an unusually good pilot.)

At last, we bumped gently. The Arabs, still over-excited,

218

opened the door and tumbled out, yelling, and were at once swallowed by a small crowd of thin, ragged, filthy scarecrows like themselves. The air leapt at me like a red-hot animal, and the sand burned through my shoes.

Here we were. We had arrived. This was The Place of Many Palms.

.   .   .

And here we are still, after two months, and I suppose I had better finish quickly.

It was no wonder that Toby's attempts to find out details about Mr. Rode had failed, because his personal affairs are a carefully guarded secret.

He is a very rich man indeed, and his money has been made over twenty years out of a strip cartoon which he invented and drew and which is syndicated all over Europe and the Americas and Great Britain. I have known it from my childhood.

He uses his wealth to finance unusual, odd, personal plans of do-gooding, and this island, this miserable place burning in its dust halfway up the Red Sea, between Arabia and Egypt, is one of them.

It used to be able to make a living, because once it really was a Place of Many Palms, and could sell dates to the villages on the mainland and had quite a little trade with them. But suddenly nearly all the water on the island dried up, and the palms died, and so the island was dying too.

Houses crumbling. No schools. Diseases. No work for the thousand or so Arabs. Nothing but dust, and flies, and despair.

Until the Rodes came. They have had a hospital built, and there is a school going up, and in the low ridge of hills that runs across the island Mr. Rode has got the Arabs digging to re-tap the water that once nourished a cedar forest there.

We live communally, in a communal house. Their daughter-in-law Ruth is here (a big girl with buck teeth but you know how Americans simply ignore being plain and very wise too) and she makes the utter best of herself, being also a qualified doctor, in white interne jackets and white skirts. I like her.

Everybody dresses like a cross between a soldier and a doctor and it really is most depressing. I was soon given the same kind of clothes, and saw no reason for declining to wear them, because if I wear my peach linen I feel wrongly dressed, and unless you do something useful, there is nothing to do. That is, nothing for which peach linen is suitable.

I am like a fish up to its fins in sand and I often seriously wonder why I don't wish I was dead.

The first evening we arrived, after the fearful sun had plopped into the flaming sea and she and I were sitting alone in the communal living-room, Mrs. Rode gave me a long talk.

Said she and Mr. R. had grown truly fond of Toby and me during the dear dead days of ancestor-hunting (oh *why* did we ever complain about *anything* then?) and decided that we were two young people who could be *fine* young people if given the chance.

Did you ever hear of such interference? (Kindly meant, but interference usually is.) And neither Toby nor I *want* to be a fine young person, we think they're the end.

So Mr. Rode, who has a peculiar sense of humour, as his cartoons show, thought up this plan for misleading us about an island near Tahiti, and sort of kidnapping us, for our own good.

She then told me that we must simply stay here, and work to help these uneducated Arabs.

It was difficult to make a fuss, because she saw the facts plainly—our helplessness, and lack of powerful friends and money—and also because she spoke so kindly and gently. I had always liked her, as you know, and even now, in this desolate place full of low characters, the fluffy, cheerful look she had, which first attracted me, shone through the medical-military clothes and comforted me.

In the fairly cool evening—cool at least compared to the unconveyable heat of the day—the soft washing of the sea came to us as we sat in the dusk. For an instant, I had a kind of dim flash in my mind that one day I would feel differently about the poor Place of Many Palms.

Mrs. Rode, after a little silence, suddenly said that God almost never made a place without at least one natural consolation. Cactus flowers, she said, and colours in the ice.

I must say I thought that saying this was the ultimate and final end. *When there* are *no shops here.*

Or at least, only stalls selling trays of things all over flies, and one dark ruined café run by an Italian who is a drunk. And who can blame him?

But just sit still for a minute, and imagine. No shops.

Quite a place, as Guy would have said.

I sulkily said that I supposed I must try to make the best of it, and Mrs. Rode patted my hand and said that the thing to do was to live from hour to hour, and then Toby came in with Mr. Rode and the others.

Mr. Cheng was born in America and returned to China to be a missionary but was scorned by the Communists and thrown out. Now he was here to make the Arabs into Christians. (I thought it would be better to make them wash. Nothing but the sea washes here.)

There is also Ed. Steegman, who drives the various jeeps and so forth over the new roads and is a dentist, and his wife Lyddy, who is a nurse. So I suppose we are well supplied with experts.

The communal house, though definitely unluxurious, is at

least clean and air-conditioned, and Toby and I have a kind of Arab bed-sitter to ourselves—with bearable bathroom and loo—(trust Americans).

I expect you will be thinking that Toby lost his reason when Mr. Rode explained to him our situation. But you never can tell, with my Toby. He shouted with laughter, startling and pleasing Mr. Rode, and said he wished old Guy had been here to see where he, Toby, had landed up.

(I think, you know, that he just *dare* not give way, but had to call upon every ounce of courage and guts he had, because the situation was so appalling.)

He had been having misgivings about our way of living, as you know, for some time, and now although the island is unimaginably depressing and the Arabs so dismal and filthy, at least we *are* under the wing of a very very rich man, who likes us, and wishes us well. For the present all uncertainty as to food and lodging and money is at an end.

That makes for a sensation of peace. Oh, and I am sure of my g.h.m. every day, although often it is not hot. (I don't go for heat much, lately)

For some weeks, I did do my best to be idle.

But it was a failure.

Partly because everyone else was busying about, washing, cleaning, swabbing, advising, building—oh, no end to it. I couldn't sit all day just writing, it began to affect me mentally, and Toby was already hopping around in shorts and topee (looking angelic) being useful to Mr. Rode——

And partly because of those Arab children.

Boiling gravy, they were neglected. I have never seen such sores and weakness and dirt. You positively had to do something about them, much as you did not want to. So I began by getting paper handkerchiefs from Lyddy, and going to the little square in the centre of the crumbling, ancient white little town where they played or lay in the shade, and wiping all their noses. Every single one.

It was a difficult task, as they simply hated it and would not tamely submit, and their mothers came shrieking out, getting over-excited and fearing the Evil Eye, and *I* feared there would be a riot.

But I persevered. And now I have twelve of them to wash, feed and wipe every day under the supervision of Ruth, given into my care by Mrs Rode, and I am beginning to feel different about them.

It is very curious.

I cannot say that I enjoy the task, which is complicated and exhausting, but when it is over—but somehow I have the growing feeling that it never is—I feel a satisfied kind of sensation.

Knowing their names and ages and parents makes a difference.

So the time does not pass too slowly, in fact, it flies, and the evenings, when we sit in the communal room and talk about our day's work and sometimes Ruth sings to her guitar or Toby makes something up to make us laugh—the evenings are something I look forward to, surprisingly.

I think Toby secretly yearns, and hopes that one day Mr. Rode will return to the world, and take us with him. But Mr. R. has already made two journeys to the mainland, to discuss business affairs by telephone, and there was not one word about our accompanying him, and I don't think Toby is unbearably unhappy. He can be his gay self, you see (my Arab babies love him) without the strain of pretending to be highly connected, and there is no doubt that he is useful to Mr. Rode. My Toby.

Don't imagine for one instant, please, that we shall be *content* to stagnate in this backwater for ever. We would sooner be in Miami or Paris—as who would not?—and Toby says that the great world shall hear of us yet. You never know what will happen and there is my father's brother in France.

But I am tired of writing.

Good-bye.